"Aw man! It says it takes *eight* hours to cook this turkey in the oven!"

"We don't have eight hours!" said Kel.

Kenan rolled his eyes. *Of course we don't have eight hours. We barely have eight* minutes.

"I know how we can cook this bird fast!" said Kenan. It was another one of Kenan's ingenious ideas. "I'm gonna shove this bird in the microwave and set it on high." With that, Kenan tried to stuff the giant turkey into the tiny microwave oven, but it wouldn't fit.

"Here! Try this!" offered Kel, handing Kenan a rolling pin. Kenan took it and pounded the turkey all the way into the microwave, slamming the door shut.

Kel, meanwhile, was reading the cookbook, and had more bad news for Kenan. "Oh, but Kenan. It says here that even in a microwave, it takes two hours to cook."

Kenan thought for a moment. Then he picked up the tiny microwave oven and threw it into the regular oven. He slammed the oven door shut, and turned it up as high as it would go. "There. That oughtta speed things up!"

Kenan & Kel™ books:

Aw, Here It Goes!
Family and Food and Orange Soda

Look for these other Nickelodeon® books:

Good Burger™
Good Burger™ 2 Go
All That™: Fresh Out the Box

Available from MINSTREL Books

KENAN & KEL ™

FAMILY AND FOOD AND ORANGE SODA

Steve Freeman

Based on the teleplays "Turkey Day"
by Alex Reid,
"Merry Christmas, Kenan"
by Dan Schneider,
and "Who Loves Orange Soda?"
by Sharon Sussman & Burt Wheeler

A MINSTREL® BOOK

Published by POCKET BOOKS
New York London Toronto Sydney Tokyo Singapore

A MINSTREL PAPERBACK *Original*

A Minstrel Book published by
POCKET BOOKS, a division of Simon & Schuster Inc.
1230 Avenue of the Americas, New York, NY 10020

ISBN: 0-671-02429-9

First Minstrel Books printing December 1998

10 9 8 7 6 5 4 3 2 1

Cover photography by Blake Little

Printed in the U.S.A.

For Rachel, Johnny, David, and Brittany.

FAMILY AND FOOD AND ORANGE SODA

AW, HERE GO THE HOLIDAYS!

As Kenan and Kel make their way out in front of the red curtain on stage, Kenan can't help noticing Kel is wearing a Pilgrim's hat and is holding a live turkey.

"Hey, everybody!" shouts Kel. "Welcome to our book." He looks over at Kenan. "How did I do, Kenan? Did ya notice how I said welcome to our 'book,' and not welcome to our 'show'? That was good, huh?" As Kel awaits praise from his pal, his turkey gobbles loudly.

"Yeah, Kel, that was great. After all, it's always good for the people to know whether they're reading a book or watching a television show. But, I have a question . . . ," asks Kenan. "What's with the funny hat and the plump bird?"

"Well," Kel begins, "since this book is about family and food and the 'holididdie-ays,' and since the first 'holididdie-ay' of the 'holididdie-ay' season is Thanksgiving, I thought it would be a good idea to wear a hat like the Pilgrim people wore who first 'thanks gave.'"

1

Kenan gives Kel a long, peculiar stare as the turkey continues to gobble. " 'Holiday' season," corrects Kenan.

"Huh?" says Kel, confused.

"You keep saying 'holididdie-ay.' Everyone on the planet except you seems to know that the word is 'holiday,' *pine cone.*"

"But I *like* to say 'holididdie-ay,' " Kel protests. "It's fun. Try it. Holididdie-ay, holididdie-ay, holididdie-ay!"

Kenan is becoming irritated. It's just the beginning of the book and Kel is already being difficult. "I'm not gonna say 'holididdie-ay!' Although . . . I do admit it *is* kind of fun," Kenan admits. "But, whyyyyyy have you seen fit to tuck a huge live turkey under your arm?"

"He's not a turkey bird. He's a long-necked chicken," argues Kel.

"Long-necked chicken? Kel, I got news for you. There's no such thing as a long-necked chicken just like there's no such word as 'holididdie-ay.' What you have there is what ya call a gobblin' *turkey . . . dumpling.*"

"Shhhhh!" admonishes Kel, as he covers what he believes to be the turkey's ears. "You'll hurt his feelings. Long-necked chickens are very sensitive."

"Well," says Kenan, staring menacingly at Kel's turkey, "then he'll be *extremely* sensitive when he hears what his role is going to be in the upcoming Thanksgiving holididdie-ay."

"What are ya talkin' about, Kenan? What's his role going to be?" Kel holds on to his turkey tightly, as Kenan licks his chops.

"Well, let's just put it this way. I hope he likes stuffing, because he's gonna be full of it."

"But Kenan, people eat turkey on the holidays, and see, James, here, is a long-necked chicken, so he's got nothing to worry about."

"James?" asks Kenan. "The bird is named James?"

"Yeah, and he's my friend," says Kel as he gently strokes his turkey. "That's why I brought him out here. To protect him from people like you during the holididdie-ay season."

Kenan can see that Kel and James have formed an attachment. True, Kenan does get rather hungry when he thinks about the holidays, but he couldn't begin to imagine actually eating a close friend of Kel's. "Don't worry, Kel," assures Kenan. "I'm not gonna eat your turkey friend. In fact, I'll help you protect him from those who would enjoy dining with him this holiday season."

"Oh, thank you, Kenan!" shouts Kel, and he gives him a big hug, almost crushing poor James, who lets out several loud gobbles of protest.

"That's okay, freak. I mean, *Kel.* We'll just keep James here on the empty stage until the book is over, then he should be safe."

"Kenan, why do people have to eat birds when they celebrate the holidays, anyway?" asks Kel, typically wide-eyed and confused.

Good question, thinks Kenan. He puts his hand to his chin and ponders it carefully. "Because, *Dippity Do,*" he finally responds, "that's what the holidays are all about. Gettin' with your family and eatin' big plump turkey birds, and stuffing, and cranberry sauce, and pumpkin pie, and hams, and yams, and jams."

"And don't forget orange soda," reminds Kel.

"Oh yeah, *how* can I forget orange soda?" asks Kenan sarcastically. "That's one of the big ones."

"Hey, Kenan?" asks Kel, he and his turkey both full of wonder. "Why do we have holidays, anyway?"

"Because," responds Kenan in a grouchy, 'how could you ask me such a silly question' tone, "people have to have *something* to celebrate. Without holidays, what reason would we have to throw huge wingdings with lots of food and presents and decorations and singin' and hollerin'?"

"Good point," says Kel. "Holididdie-ays give the people something to look forward to."

"Exactly," agrees Kenan. "That's why the holiday season is such a big deal. You wait all year, and then you get those three really big holidays right there in a row—"

"Yeah, I know," interrupts Kel. "Presidents' Day, the Fourth of July, and Halloween."

"No, *pimento!* I'm talking about Thanksgiving, Christmas, and New Year's!" shouts Kenan. If he didn't know Kel better, he'd be amazed by Kel's ignorance, but he knows Kel, and this response is no surprise to him.

"Oh, yeah," says Kel. "Those are pretty big ones too."

"They sure are," says Kenan. "See, then all of a sudden, the people go crazy with the joy and the eating of food. They don't have to go to work, so they start making travel plans to see family members that they've tried to avoid talking to all year long."

"Yeah, and then they start decorating their living rooms and handing out caramels," offers Kel.

"Yep," says Kenan. "And they get all affectionate and warm and loving toward one another, and then they make with all the well-wishing and the football games."

"Right," says Kel. "And then they start talking about what a happy, healthy year the next year's gonna be, and then it starts all over again come November."

"That's what we're talking about in this book," says Kenan. "We're gonna talk about Thanksgiving, Christmas, and New Year's, and all the joy they bring. We'll start by talkin' about Thanksgiving. Do you know when the very first Thanksgiving was, Kel?"

"Sure," responds Kel confidently. "It was way back in nineteen sixty-four. The Indians gave the overdressed Pilgrim people free corn on the cob and discount auto parts. The overdressed Pilgrim people gave the Indians some turkey birds, pistachio ice cream, and some golf clubs and they all got together and had a late lunch. And I think there were some Spanish dancers, but I'll have to look it up."

James, the turkey, emits a confused-sounding gobble. Kenan simply stares at Kel, his mouth wide open in shock. "Were you sick a lot in the third grade?" asks Kenan.

"Not that I know of," says Kel.

"Well, you're sick now," says Kenan. "Get some help."

"Okay," says Kel, and he and his turkey start to walk away.

"Not now, *flapjack!*" shouts Kenan. "Go get help *after* the book. We got stories to tell about family and food!"

Kel and his turkey turn around and come back. "I love holididdie-ay stories! Are we gonna tell 'em about the Thanksgiving I accidentally spilled cranberry sauce down your grandma?" asks Kel, tightly clutching his turkey.

"Nope," says Kenan. "I don't think we'll tell them about that Thanksgiving."

"Well, how about the Thanksgiving you accidentally slapped your daddy with a ham?" asks Kel with an ear-to-ear smile. Recalling the ham-slapping incident clearly makes him happy.

"No," says Kenan. "I don't think we'll tell 'em about that Thanksgiving either."

"Well, then what Thanksgiving are we gonna tell the people about?" asks Kel, his turkey now gobbling loudly.

"I think we'll tell 'em about the worst Thanksgiving of all," says Kenan, starting to walk away.

"You mean the one where we? . . ." asks Kel, frightened even to think about it.

Kenan nods his head. "Yep. That's the one." And with that, Kenan walks away.

FAMILY AND FOOD AND ORANGE SODA

"Naw, Kenan!" shouts Kel. "Not that one! I don't wanna tell the people about *that* Thanksgiving! Please, Kenan! Can't we tell 'em about another one? Kenan! Kenan? Nooooo!" Kel gazes in desperation at his turkey friend, James. "Aw, here go the holidays!" shouts Kel, and he and his turkey run off after Kenan.

"TURKEY DAY"

Sheryl Rockmore walked into the kitchen, put on oven mitts, and began to open the oven. "Roger, you want me to baste the turkey?" she shouted out to her husband.

Although Roger Rockmore is a caring, gentle man, and a good father to Kenan and Kyra, if you didn't already know him and you were to see him for the first time, you might be a little afraid of him. After all, he's an awfully large, intimidating man with a shaved bald head and serious eyes behind severe-looking glasses. So, he would be the last man you'd expect to see wearing his wife's dainty little apron over his shirt and vest. But, sure enough, he was wearing just that, as he raced into the kitchen to check on his turkey.

"Nooo!" he yelled. "Don't touch my turkey! I'm in charge of cooking the Thanksgiving turkey, and only *I* may baste it!"

"Okay!" replied Sheryl, somewhat taken aback. She

took off the mitts and straightened her flower-print dress. "Don't get your underwear in a bunch."

Sheryl knew it was Thanksgiving, and on Thanksgiving, people who don't normally do the cooking are suddenly transformed into master turkey chefs. This was the case with Roger. He was proud of his turkey and had worked very hard to prepare it. He opened the oven with loving care, grabbed the large baster, and gazed inside at the roasting bird.

"Hello, mister turkey lurkey!" said Roger lovingly, as he reached inside the oven and gently squeezed the baster over his prize turkey. He was talking to it the way a dad would talk to his newborn child. Frankly, it was a little weird.

At that moment, Kel and Kenan burst through the back door.

"Happy Thanksgiving!" shouted Kel, the moment they walked in. This sudden commotion startled Roger and caused him to slam the oven door on his hand.

"Ow!" Roger immediately stormed around the kitchen in pain. He quickly opened the freezer door, grabbed a couple of ice cubes, and applied them to his injured hand.

Kel, noticing Roger's pretty apron, couldn't let it go. In his dark T-shirt, and wearing his customary beret pulled back on his forehead, Kel followed Roger around the kitchen.

"Ooh, that's a nice pretty dress you got there, Mister Rockmore! *Ooh!* Will you go with me to the school dance?"

"Kel," replied Roger, who didn't really see the humor, "if you don't keep your mouth closed, I'm gonna *dance* all over your—"

"Oooh!" Kenan exclaimed peering into the oven, admiring his dad's turkey. "This turkey smells good!"

Roger rushed to the aid of his masterpiece. "Both of you vultures keep away from my turkey bird!" he warned. "I've been cooking it for over seven hours and I want it to be absolutely perfect for Thanksgiving dinner." With that, Roger opened the oven, carefully removed the large pan containing the giant, freshly basted turkey, and set it lightly on the counter. And a fine-looking turkey it was. Kenan and Kel drooled over the glistening, perfectly golden brown bird and the incredible aroma. "And don't breathe on it!" cautioned Roger.

"Roger, honey," Sheryl interrupted his turkey worship to remind her husband that they were running late.

"Aw, did Aunt Bertha puff up again?" asked Kenan.

"Uh-huh," Sheryl replied. "She's *all* puffy. We have to go see her in the hospital today."

Kel appeared confused. He was thinking about all the things that could possibly make Aunt Bertha puffy.

"All right, Kenan," said Sheryl, as she and Roger made their way out the door, "I started setting the dinner table. You finish it up for me, okay?"

"Yes, ma'am," said Kenan, as they headed into the living room. Kenan noticed the dinner table was set for eight people, and he asked his mom who was coming for Thanksgiving dinner.

"I'm invited, right?" asked Kel. Kenan and Kel then celebrated Kel's invitation by banging fists together.

"What about *your* family?" asked Roger, annoyed at the prospect of sharing Thanksgiving dinner—and especially his turkey—with Kel.

"Well, I'm going to eat with my family *after* I eat with your family," replied Kel cheerfully. This seemed like a perfectly fine idea to Kel. He was certainly going to get the most out of this Thanksgiving. There wasn't a doubt in his mind about his ability to eat two Thanksgiving dinners, one right after the other.

"Kenan, there'll be eight of us," said Sheryl. "Our family, Kel, Grandma Molly, Uncle Raymond, and Aunt Gerdie."

"Aw, Aunt Gerdie?" asked Kenan in a disappointed tone.

"What's wrong with Aunt Gerdie?" asked Kel.

"The woman has a full-grown mustache!" exclaimed Kenan in disgust.

Sheryl gave Kenan a disapproving glare. "Kenan!" The fact that Kenan was still a kid was the problem, here. Even though adults realize Aunt Gerdie has a full-grown mustache, they somehow manage to pretend they don't notice and are able to avoid mentioning it. It's called maturity. Kenan wasn't ready to mature *that* quickly.

"How am I supposed to eat my Thanksgiving dinner

11

when I'm staring at a woman who looks like she's got a big ol' hairy caterpillar crawling under her nose?" asked Kenan angrily.

Kel had a good idea. He suggested that when Aunt Gerdie came, maybe they should shave her.

"No!" Roger shouted. *"Neither* of you will shave Aunt Gerdie."

"And look, Kenan," added Sheryl, "no comments about her mustache. And just don't mess up the house, okay?"

"Hey, Kel," Kenan joked. "Go get that bucket of mud."

Roger still didn't see the humor.

"I'm just joking," reassured their son. "You two have fun at the hospital."

"Yeah," added Kel, as Sheryl and Roger made their way out the front door. "Give your puffy Aunt Bertha my best." After Sheryl and Roger left the house, Kel turned to Kenan with a look of unmistakable anticipation. "Man, I can't wait to meet your hairy aunt."

"Trust me," said Kenan. "It's not a pretty picture. Now come on and help me set the table."

"Cool," replied Kel, and they both headed back into the kitchen.

"You get the water glasses. I'll meet you out in the dining room," instructed Kenan, as he grabbed a handful of silverware.

Kel opened the cabinet and took out a few glasses while Kenan made his way back to the table. As Kel began to follow Kenan out the door, he turned and noticed the beautiful golden brown turkey waiting patiently on the counter, ready to be devoured by eight people. Kel gazed lovingly at the bird and licked his lips. He moved slowly toward the turkey. He placed his nose gently over it and sniffed, taking in its mouthwatering aroma. He stood there and fantasized a moment about eating Roger's turkey. He couldn't resist. He reached over and pinched just the tiniest piece off the turkey and put it quickly in his mouth.

Kel was on his way to turkey heaven.

His journey, however, was rudely interrupted.

"Hey, Kel! Come on!" shouted Kenan from the dining room.

Kel quickly swallowed his tiny piece of turkey and ran out the door, into the dining room, where he found Kenan placing silverware on the table. Kel began setting down the water glasses.

"Okay, we need bread plates. I'll get them," said Kenan.

"No, I'll get 'em!" Kel quickly volunteered, as if there was a sense of urgency.

"Okay," Kenan replied, somewhat surprised by Kel's sudden desire to help out. *"You* get the bread plates."

Kel immediately scurried back into the kitchen. He glanced at his love—the turkey—as he made his way toward the cabinet where the plates were. The cabinets in the Rockmore kitchen had glass doors, and as Kel reached for the bread plates, he gazed at the turkey through the cabinet, and his hungry breath began to fog the glass. Once again, he couldn't resist, and he walked across the kitchen to the turkey. Kel's problem was, he had no self-control. Kel glanced around nervously, then quickly ripped off another tiny piece.

"Ohhhh . . ." said Kel, in the midst of turkey ecstasy. Then, he reached over and tore off another piece, this one a little bigger than the first two. Then, still not satisfied, Kel put his hand on one of the turkey legs. He was about to pinch off another piece when suddenly Kenan shouted from the other room.

"Kel! We haven't got all day!"

This startled Kel so much that he flinched. His hand still on the turkey leg, he accidentally ripped the entire turkey leg off the roasted bird! He gasped. Still chewing his last piece, he quickly tried to stick the leg back on the turkey, but it kept falling off. It was at that moment that Kenan entered the kitchen. Kel quickly placed his body in front of the turkey so Kenan wouldn't see it.

"Kel, man, where are those bread plates? Oh, forget it. I'll get 'em," said Kenan, not noticing that Kel had just shoved a whole turkey leg into his pocket. Kenan walked over to the cabinet and grabbed a handful of bread plates. "Grab some soup spoons, will ya?" asked Kenan.

"Mmmm-hmmm," replied Kel, his mouth still full of the Rockmores' turkey.

When Kenan left to go back into the dining room, Kel breathed a sigh of relief. What was he to do, now? He thought for a moment. There was no way he would be able to successfully put the turkey's leg back on the turkey. Therefore, the logical decision was to get rid of the evidence. He began to ravenously devour the turkey leg. It was delicious, and it was then that Kel realized it was all over. Kel pulled up a chair from the kitchen table and sat next to the counter.

"Oh, it's *on!*" Kel said to himself, and he began to eat the entire turkey. "Ohhh! Good turkey!" he exclaimed, chewing rapidly. "Mmmm! Awwww! Mmmm!" Kel didn't have a care in the world. He had finally gained admittance into turkey heaven.

Kenan's little sister, Kyra, looked pretty in her red dress as she ran downstairs into the living room, excited about Thanksgiving dinner. Kenan was still setting the table.

"Hey, Kenan, whatcha doing?" she asked her big brother.

"What's it look like I'm doing? I'm setting the table," he responded in a big-brotherly, grouchy tone.

"Yeah. Well, you're setting it wrong," said Kyra. Kenan, confident he was doing a perfectly fine job, couldn't imagine what he could be doing wrong. "The water glasses go over the knife, not the forks. Duh!" teased Kyra. Kyra was just being a little sister. Whenever a little sister has an opportunity to point out when her big brother is wrong, it should be enjoyed to the fullest.

"Yeah?" said Kenan. "Well I say the water glasses go on the . . ." Kenan suddenly heard a strange noise coming from the kitchen. Kyra heard it too. It sounded like someone loudly chomping on food. "Do you hear something?" Kenan asked his sister.

"Yeah," said Kyra, listening. "What *is* that?"

Kenan wasn't sure. He only knew it was a sound he had heard before. He thought for a moment. *Where* had he heard this sound before? He began to remember. It was on a documentary he'd watched on TV about wild animals eating their prey. Realizing this was indeed that same sound, Kenan's eyes widened in horror. "Noooooooo!" he screamed.

"What?" asked Kyra, frightened by Kenan's fear.

Kenan immediately flung open the shutters that separated the dining room from the kitchen and peered through.

"Eeeeeeeeeeeeee!" squealed Kenan, as he looked into the kitchen. There was his pal, Kel, sitting at the counter, resting comfortably after having just eaten Roger Rockmore's entire masterpiece turkey.

Kenan and Kyra raced into the kitchen. All that was left of the turkey was the bony carcass. The rest of it was inside Kel, his face covered with turkey bits and turkey juice.

At that moment Kel let loose a loud, satisfied burp.

"Ohhhh noooo!" cried Kenan, as he picked up the bony remains of the turkey. "Whyyyyyyyyyyy?"

Kel was almost in tears with guilt and desperation. "I'm sorreee!"

Kenan was furious and was about to yell at Kel, but this would not be allowed by his sister, Kyra. Kyra had always had a giant crush on Kel, and since he was the love of her life, she wasn't about to let him be mistreated by her big brother.

"Kenan, don't you yell at Kel!" she warned, as she gently stroked Kel's head.

Kenan was shocked to see that Kyra would protect Kel after what he'd done. "Do you all realize what Pop's going to do to us when he sees this?" Kenan asked, beginning to panic. "We gotta do something! We gotta fix it!"

Kyra was much more calm and practical than Kenan at this point. "How are you going to fix that turkey?" she asked. "It's in Kel's stomach."

Kenan thought about this long and hard. Suddenly realizing there was nothing left to do, he quickly grabbed Kel from behind and squeezed hard, trying to force the turkey out of him. "You're going to give me my turkey back, that's what you're gonna do!" yelled Kenan. "Cough it up! Gimme my daddy's turkey back! Give it!"

"You're squeezing my pancreas!" yelled Kel.

It didn't work, and Kel fell to the kitchen floor in a heap. Kenan stood over him and pointed a finger at his friend.

"Kel, you have *really* done it this time. You have really done it!"

At that exact moment, the doorbell rang.

"Aw, your daddy's back!" Kel shouted. "Tell my momma I loved her!"

Kenan realized his parents couldn't possibly be back

17

already and they wouldn't ring the doorbell. He knew it had to be his relatives. "Kyra, go let them in, but don't let them in the kitchen."

As Kyra ran into the living room to get the door, Kenan paced back and forth through the kitchen, trying to get his thoughts together. "Okay, let's just calm down and think this through rationally," he said, holding up the turkey carcass. "Okay, we have the turkey bones, but no turkey *meat*. So, all we have to do . . ." Kenan paused and thought some more. ". . . is put some turkey meat back on the bones. Right?"

"Uh-huh," replied Kel, so desperate that he was willing to agree with anything.

"Okay!" Kenan shouted, and they went right to the refrigerator and looked inside.

"Here's two packages of sliced turkey meat!" said Kel.

"Cool!" replied Kenan, and they raced back to the pan containing the turkey bones, where Kenan frantically ripped open the packages of turkey meat. They then began slapping pieces of sliced turkey onto the carcass. After they had used up both packages, they took a step back and looked at their handiwork. It did not exactly look convincing.

"Awww! It looks *diseased!*" said Kel.

Kenan couldn't understand. He thought for sure this idea would work. What could've gone wrong? "I think it's because the turkey meat is all slicey," he reasoned. "We have to get it to look more like fresh, unsliced meat." He thought for a moment, then . . . "The food processor!'' he shouted triumphantly. There was a big food processor on the counter next to what used to be the turkey. Kenan told Kel that if they just threw the sliced meat in there and ground it all up, they could simply mold it back on the turkey. Kel agreed this was a good idea, so they tossed in the sliced turkey meat and turned on the food processor. There was a loud buzzing sound as the turkey meat whirled around in the dome of the processor.

"Okay, now we just mold this meat back onto the bones," instructed Kenan.

"Got it," said Kel, and the two of them scooped handfuls of the nasty turkey goo and tried unsuccessfully to shape it back onto the carcass.

Immediately realizing this wasn't going to work, they both began to cry.

"It's not looking very good!" said Kel, in tears.

"I'm aware!" cried Kenan, as he dumped their experiment, carcass and all, into the trash can. "Aw, *man!* My daddy's gonna kill us!"

"Bye!" shouted Kel, and he ran for the back door, but Kenan stopped him.

"Where are *you* going?" Kenan asked, grabbing onto Kel.

"Australia."

"Why?" asked Kenan.

"Because your daddy's not in Australia," replied Kel.

In the living room, Kyra had her hands full. Grandma Molly and Uncle Raymond were taking off their coats.

"Oh, Kyra! You have grown a foot since the last time I saw you!" said Grandma Molly.

"No she hasn't," crowed Uncle Raymond. "She had two feet the last time you saw her and she's got two feet now."

"I meant, she's grown a foot *taller,*" said Grandma Molly.

"Blah blah blah," said Uncle Raymond, handing his coat to Kyra and walking toward the dining room table. "Who cares? Where's the turkey? I didn't come here to yap. I came here to eat some turkey."

Uncle Raymond certainly appeared wise and dignified with his gray beard and his three-piece suit, but Kyra knew he was really nothing but a hungry grouch.

"So, where's Aunt Gerdie?" asked Kyra, trying to change the subject. Uncle Raymond informed her that they had run over a nail coming in the driveway, and she was out there changing the flat tire.

"By herself?" Kyra asked.

"Well, you know the woman," said Uncle Raymond. "She's more man than I am. Now, where's the turkey?" demanded Uncle Raymond. Kyra knew this wasn't going to be easy.

Back in the kitchen, Kenan and Kel were thinking hard. Roger and Sheryl were due back from the hospital in less than an hour, and there was no turkey to serve their guests.

"I got it!" shouted Kenan, once again. "We'll just call

up and have a fresh turkey delivered! Ha ha!" He laughed at the simplicity of his solution.

Unfortunately, it was one of those rare instances where Kel showed some common sense, and this would ruin Kenan's feeling of relief. "But it's Thanksgiving," said Kel. "Won't every place be closed?"

Kenan grabbed Kel by the shoulders and looked into his eyes with a sense of serious urgency. "We-have-to-try!" he said, pronouncing each word carefully, making sure Kel understood. "Give me that phone book!"

They began desperately flipping through the yellow pages.

"Ooh, look!" said Kel. "It says 'brassieres.'" Kel laughed. Normally, Kenan would join Kel in a laugh over the word "brassieres," but not now. There was a crisis that needed solving. Kenan slapped Kel's hand away from the phone book.

Uncle Raymond sat impatiently at the dining room table. Kyra was trying her best to hold down the fort and keep his mind off turkey. Grandma Molly was already sound asleep on the sofa, snoring loudly.

"Hey, Uncle Raymond," said Kyra, "I got all As in school last semester." *This,* Kyra thought, *is sure to impress Uncle Raymond.*

"Whoop-dee-doo," replied Uncle Raymond sarcastically. "I want some turkey."

"Well, Mom and Dad should be home real soon," said Kyra, hoping it would appease her cranky, turkey-minded relative.

"What am I supposed to do until then?" he asked. When Kyra suggested she show him some of her karate moves, Uncle Raymond replied, "Yeah. Why don't you karate chop me a turkey sandwich?"

It was no use. Uncle Raymond had a one-track mind, and it would only be a matter of time before his patience ran out.

Kenan stood in the kitchen, dialing number after number. "Every place is closed!" Kenan complained.

Kel sat on the counter and continued to look through the phone book. "Wait! You haven't tried this place!" he said, pointing to an entry in the phone book. "And it's real close. Try this place."

Kenan looked at the number and dialed. Finally, after a few rings, someone answered.

"Hello?" said Kenan, into the phone. "Are you guys open today? You are? . . . And you have turkeys? And you deliver, too?" Kenan waited for the response. "Ha! All right!" yelled Kenan, and then he smiled at Kel. It seemed their troubles were over. "I would like two large turkeys delivered to my house."

Kenan then gave them his address with a huge sigh of relief. Soon, the turkeys would be delivered, and Kenan and Kel, thanks to Kenan's genius, would be off the hook.

Kel was typically confused.

"Why'd you order two turkeys?" he asked.

"In case something bad happens to one of them," explained Kenan.

"What bad could happen?" asked Kel.

"You!"

Back in the living room, Grandma Molly was still snoring wildly on the sofa. Kyra, meanwhile, was forced to resort to extreme measures. She was attempting to entertain Uncle Raymond with some of her karate moves. Donning her white karate robe and purple belt, she carried on her demonstration in front of an angry, bored, and underfed Uncle Raymond.

"Hiii-yaaaa!" yelled Kyra, as she demonstrated her back kick. "And this is a left jab," she continued, as she performed a left jab.

"That's very nice," said Uncle Raymond, completely uninterested. "If I weren't so hungry, I'd clap."

Kenan and Kel, now happy and relieved, came in from the kitchen to save the day. "Hey, Uncle Raymond. How are you?" greeted Kenan.

"Hungry," replied Uncle Raymond angrily.

Kenan told Uncle Raymond not to worry, and assured him that they'll have *plenty* of turkey *real* soon. Then he introduced him to Kel.

"Is he a turkey?" asked Uncle Raymond.

What a strange question, thought Kenan. *And yet, so close to the truth.* "No," replied Kenan. "Kel is not a turkey."

"Then who cares?" asked Uncle Raymond. It became apparent to Kenan and Kel that Uncle Raymond wanted turkey, and he wanted it now. Trying to be a good host, Kenan said hello to Grandma Molly, only to

23

find her sound asleep on the sofa, snoring louder than ever. This was certainly turning out to be a strange Thanksgiving.

"Well, uh, where's Aunt Gerdie?" asked Kenan nervously.

"Is the turkey ready?" asked Uncle Raymond. He could think of nothing else.

At that moment, the doorbell rang, and Kenan ran to answer it. He opened the door and in walked Aunt Gerdie, mustache and all.

"Kenan!" she yelled happily. She looked very much like a normal, garden-variety aunt. She had on a purple print dress and a bright gold necklace. Her hair was gray, and her mustache was surprisingly full. Kenan was convinced that there were a lot of grown *men* who couldn't grow a mustache that hairy.

Kel stood at the end of the room, and winced in fear and disgust. "Yaagghh! Somebody get the hedge clippers!" yelled Kel, causing Kenan to give him a dirty look.

"Hey, Aunt Gerdie," said Kenan, grudgingly. For obvious reasons, he was not happy to see her.

"Give me a big kiss!" insisted Aunt Gerdie.

"I'd rather not," replied Kenan, grimacing with disgust. Aunt Gerdie didn't care. She grabbed Kenan and planted a big kiss right on his cheek. There was nothing Kenan could do but grin and bear it.

Well, during the holidays, it wasn't unusual to hear bells, and bells were ringing like crazy at the Rockmore household. This time it was the back doorbell. Kenan and Kel knew immediately who it was. Kenan told his guests to make themselves comfortable.

"I'll be comfortable when I get some turkey in my gut," said Uncle Raymond, as Kenan and Kel darted into the kitchen.

Jarvis Lode was a dumpy sort of fellow. He wore big brown overalls over a plaid shirt, and he wore an old gray baseball cap. He had a strong Southern accent, and he carried a clipboard as he stood in the back doorway of the Rockmores' kitchen.

"Howdy! My name's Jarvis!" he announced. "Jarvis Lode. Somebody here ordered two turkeys?"

"Yeah! Yeah! We did!" said Kenan, excited to be getting this ordeal over with.

"Well, I got 'em right 'cheer," replied Jarvis. "Hang on. I'll get 'em." Jarvis went outside to get the turkeys.

Kenan was relieved. "Man, Kel, we really lucked out this time!" Kenan and Kel high-fived each other as Kenan went to get the empty pan that had once contained the turkey Kel had devoured. "I'll just put one of the turkeys in this same pan, and my dad will never know the difference."

It was then that Kenan heard another rather peculiar sound. It was the sound of two *live* turkeys gobbling loudly as they entered his kitchen.

"I think your daddy's gonna know the difference," observed Kel, looking at the birds as they waddled through the kitchen.

"Jarvis?" said Kenan.

"Yessir?" asked Jarvis.

"Partner, these turkeys are *alive,*" said Kenan in a disappointed tone.

It soon became clear that Jarvis was not the brightest man around. "Yep," he replied. "You sure do know your turkeys, don'tcha?"

As the confused turkeys roamed through the Rockmore kitchen, Kenan tried to explain to Jarvis that he didn't ask for live turkeys at all. "No," Kenan explained, "we wanted our turkeys golden brown and ready to eat."

"Well," replied Jarvis, as he made his way out the door. "You better get to it, then. I'll send ya a bill. Happy Thanksgiving!"

"No, it isn't!" screamed Kenan after him, but Jarvis was already gone. Kenan then turned to Kel. He was fresh out of ideas. "What are we gonna do, now?"

"Well," began Kel, pointing to the turkeys, "I think we should name this one Tootie, and this one Regine."

There was no time for Kenan to be irritated. He could hear Uncle Raymond screaming from the living room. "Hey! Do I get to eat some turkey or don't I? Kenan?"

"Uncle Raymond's coming! Quick! Hide the turkeys!" alerted Kenan. He and Kel began chasing Tootie and Regine around the kitchen. Finally, they were able to usher the turkeys into the pantry and shut the door behind them just as Uncle Raymond entered. Kenan and Kel leaned against the refrigerator and pretended to be nonchalant.

"I don't mean to be rude," began Uncle Raymond,

"but if I don't get some turkey soon, I'm leavin' this dump!"

Once again, Kenan had to reassure Uncle Raymond, telling him they would have some turkey real soon. Suddenly, Uncle Raymond could hear gobbling sounds from inside the pantry.

"I'm so hungry, I'm starting to *hear* turkeys!" exclaimed Uncle Raymond.

"Ha! Oh, funny, Uncle Raymond!" replied Kenan nervously. "Gobble gobble! Heh heh . . ." Kenan had to think fast. It was only a matter of time before his starving Uncle Raymond would discover the live turkeys in the pantry, and that there was no cooked turkey for him to eat. He called for Kyra to come into the kitchen and take Uncle Raymond back into the living room with his sleeping Grandma Molly and his hairy-faced Aunt Gerdie.

"Aw, this stinks!" complained Uncle Raymond, as Kyra dragged him out of the kitchen.

Time was running out. Soon, Kenan's mom and dad would be home from visiting his puffy Aunt Bertha, and . . . well, Kenan didn't even want to think about what his dad would do. It was too painful. "Now what do we do?" asked Kenan. "Every store with turkeys is going to be closed . . ." Suddenly, Kenan stopped. He had another idea. Normally, Kel wasn't too fond of Kenan's ideas, but any idea of Kenan's had to be better than the idea of having to face Mr. Rockmore if he came home to find out about the fate of his prize turkey. "Rigby's!" shouted Kenan.

Of course, Rigby's Grocery Store. Why didn't Kenan think of that before? After all, he worked there, and he had the keys. Kenan and Kel grabbed their coats and raced out the back door over to Rigby's.

Chris Potter was the manager of Rigby's Grocery Store, and he had just closed it for the Thanksgiving holiday. He was standing at the counter of the small neighborhood store, filling a large grocery bag full of eggs. "There," he said. "Mother will certainly enjoy these raw eggs," he said to himself. Then, he put on his coat, turned out the light, and was just about to leave the store with his bag of eggs when Kenan and Kel burst in. *Wham!* They knocked Chris flat, his eggs flying everywhere.

"Ooh, Chris! Sorry!" said Kenan, as he and Kel helped Chris up.

Chris was certainly not expecting to see them. "What are you guys doing? You knocked me all down! Ohhh . . . I'm all eggy!" Chris complained.

"Chris!" said Kenan, urgently. "We need a turkey!"

"Well, hurry up," demanded Chris. "I'm taking mother to the Thanksgiving dinner at Les Meats."

Kenan and Kel didn't care where Chris was taking his mother. It didn't matter. The only thing that *did* matter was getting a turkey and cooking it as soon as possible. "Well, that's very nice, Chris." Kenan and Kel rushed to the frozen food section and pulled out a huge turkey. "Bye!" said Kenan, and he and Kel rushed toward the door with their frozen turkey.

"Wait a minute! You have to help me clean this up!" shouted Chris, as he chased them toward the door.

But Kenan and Kel could not be bothered with cleaning up the mess. They rushed out the door, slamming it shut right on Chris's nose, leaving him in great pain.

Kenan and Kel rushed through the back door into the Rockmores' kitchen, and threw off their coats. "Hand me that cookbook!" ordered Kenan, as he slammed the frozen turkey down on the counter.

Kel grabbed the cookbook off the shelf and began casually flipping through it. "Hmmm," said Kel, turning the pages at a painfully slow pace. "Rump roast . . . soup . . . squash . . ."

Kenan was about to lose his mind. "Gimme that book! We don't have a lot of time, schmo!" Kenan flipped through the cookbook until he found the turkey section. "Aw man!" cried Kenan in a discouraging tone. "It says it takes *eight* hours to cook this turkey in the oven!"

"We don't have eight hours!" said Kel.

Kenan rolled his eyes. *Of course we don't have eight hours. We barely have eight minutes.*

"I know how we can cook this bird fast!" said Kenan. It was another one of Kenan's ingenious ideas. He rushed the turkey over to the microwave. "I'm gonna shove this bird in the microwave and set it on high." With that, Kenan tried to stuff the giant turkey into the tiny microwave oven, but it wouldn't fit. "Kel, hand me a lubricant," he shouted.

Kel reached into the cabinet, pulled out a bottle of corn oil, and handed it to Kenan.

Kenan poured the corn oil all over the turkey, and shoved it into the microwave. "It's almost in!" he yelled.

"Here! Try this!" offered Kel, handing Kenan a rolling pin. Kenan took it and pounded the turkey all the way into the microwave, slamming the door shut.

Kel, meanwhile, was reading the cookbook, and had more bad news for Kenan.

"Oh, but Kenan. It says here that even in a microwave, it takes two hours to cook."

Kenan thought for a moment. He then picked up the tiny microwave oven and threw it into the regular oven. He slammed the oven door shut, and turned it up as high as it would go. "There. That oughtta speed things up!" said Kenan, wiping his hands together after a job well done.

"Yeah," agreed Kel. Both boys smiled proudly over Kenan's latest stroke of genius. Finally, it seemed as if they were out of the woods. And, why not? After all, if it only took two hours to cook the turkey in the microwave oven, it seemed one would only need a little help to speed up the process. So, putting the microwave oven with the turkey cooking inside it, *inside* the regular oven turned all the way up, was a perfectly brilliant idea. Wasn't it? The way Kenan and Kel saw it, the turkey should be all cooked up in about fifteen minutes.

Yessiree, a perfectly brilliant idea.

Back in the Rockmore living room, Kyra was still attempting to entertain her bored, restless relatives with more of her karate moves. She set up a thick wooden board over two concrete blocks, yelled, "Hiiii-yaaaa!" and smashed the board clean in half with her tiny little fist. It was amazing!

However, Uncle Raymond was still unimpressed, Grandma Molly was still asleep, and Aunt Gerdie just sat there, stroking her mustache.

Suddenly, the silence was broken by a loud explosion that came from the kitchen. Smoke filled the living room, as Kyra sprinted into the kitchen to see what had happened. There she found Kenan and Kel, veiled behind thick, dark gray smoke. They were in shock, their clothes tattered and ripped apart by the explosion. The kitchen was a total mess, and the oven door had blown completely off.

"Any more ideas?" asked Kel, as the ruined turkey dropped from the ceiling and landed on the kitchen table, right next to them.

Kyra took all this in, and gasped. "What? . . ."

"Just hush!" interrupted Kenan, his voice completely worn out from the ordeal. "Kyra, we'll be right back! I got one more idea."

Yes, it was true. His clothes burnt to a crisp, covered

with smoke, Kenan Rockmore had one more idea. "Where did Chris say he was taking his mom for Thanksgiving dinner?" Kenan asked Kel. *It's funny how quickly things can change, isn't it?* Kenan thought. *Suddenly, it* was *important to know where Chris was taking his mom to dinner. Suddenly, it was* very *important.*

Kel thought hard. "Uhh . . . Les Meats, I think it was called."

"Yeah, that's it," said Kenan. "Let's go!"

Kyra surveyed the kitchen as Kenan and Kel headed for the back door. "What about this mess?" she asked.

"Just clean up the mess," instructed her brother, sounding as if he were about to pass out from shock and exhaustion. "We'll be back, and don't let anybody in the kitchen." With that, Kenan grabbed Kel's arm, and they headed out the door. Kyra grabbed a broom and began sweeping, failing to notice the two live turkeys who were now waddling happily about in the smoke-filled kitchen.

Thanksgiving was a busy night at Les Meats. It seemed like all the people in Chicago who didn't feel like *cooking* turkey had come there to *eat* turkey. It was a fancy restaurant, and Kenan and Kel were anything but properly dressed when they stumbled in, in their shredded, burnt clothes. The maitre d' was not happy to see them. "Yes, may I help you . . . *gentlemen?*" he asked in an annoyed, haughty tone.

"Yeah," said Kenan. "We need a turkey."

"Yeah," replied Kel. "Preferably one that's dead and cooked."

The maitre d' chuckled. "Today is Thanksgiving," he informed Kenan and Kel, as if they didn't know. "If you want a turkey, it must be ordered two full days in advance. They take eight hours to cook."

"So I've heard," said Kenan.

It was then that Kel spotted Chris, dressed in a coat and tie, sitting alone at a table for two. Much to the disappointment of the maitre d', who didn't want his dinner guests to be disgusted by the sight of Kenan and Kel's shabby appearance, the boys rushed onto the dining room floor and over to Chris's table.

Chris was shocked to see them. *Especially* in the condition they were in. "What are you two doing here?" he demanded. "And why are your clothes all betattered?"

"'Betattered?'" repeated Kenan and Kel in unison. That was a word they had never heard before. But it wasn't unlike Chris Potter to make up new words. He seemed to enjoy adding the letters B-E to words that didn't really need them.

"Forget it," said Chris. "Now, what do you want? My mother is in the bathroom, putting in her 'meat teeth,' and I don't want you here when she gets back. You're both covered with filth!"

Just then, a waiter came over and set down a large silver platter with a beautiful silver dome on top of it.

"Here's your turkey, sir," said the waiter, as he lifted the dome off the platter, revealing a delicious-looking, golden brown turkey.

"Oh, what a beautiful bird!" exclaimed Chris, as the waiter walked away.

Kenan and Kel took one look at each other and knew what they had to do. Kenan quickly took the gravy container from the table, and pretended to *accidentally* dump its contents on Chris's lap.

Chris was incensed—not to mention, wet. *"Doooh!* You got gravy all over my trousers!" he yelled.

"Sorry, Chris," said Kenan, giving his best fake apology. "Let me help clean that up."

Kenan then turned Chris around and helped wipe Chris's pants with the tablecloth while nodding slyly to Kel. Kel took the cue. With Chris completely distracted, Kel quickly grabbed the turkey and stuffed it into his shirt.

"Bye, Chris! Happy Thanksgiving!" said Kenan, and he and Kel sped toward the front door of the restaurant, past their friend the maitre d'.

"Don't tell nobody!" Kel warned the maitre d', as they headed out the door, the hot turkey sticking out of Kel's ripped shirt.

Kenan and Kel rushed back into the Rockmores' kitchen. There was no time to lose. Kel raced over to the pan on the counter, opened up his shirt, and dropped the stolen, freshly cooked, delectable golden brown turkey into the pan.

"We got it! Ha ha!" laughed Kenan. He looked through the shutters into the living room to find Kyra, Uncle Raymond, Grandma Molly, and Aunt Gerdie all still sitting there, waiting. "And my parents still aren't home. We're cool!" bragged Kenan, suddenly realizing he needed to sit down. It had been a difficult, scary ordeal, but it was finally over. Kenan and Kel had managed to replace the turkey, stolen or not. There it was, sitting there in its pan on the counter, ready to be admired and eaten by eight Thanksgiving dinner guests, just like Roger had left it. Both Kenan and Kel breathed a sigh of relief.

"I need some orange soda," said Kel. He reached into the Rockmores' refrigerator. After the mess they had just gotten out of, Kel felt he deserved to celebrate with his all-time favorite beverage. He gazed lovingly at the bright orange liquid. "Who loves orange soda?" asked Kel.

Oh, no! Kel's launching into his "orange soda routine." Kenan had heard it so many times before, but, as if there was some unwritten rule, he had no choice but to cooperate. "Aw, here it goes," moaned Kenan.

"Kel loves orange soda," continued Kel.

"Is it *true?"* asked Kenan in a sarcastic tone.

"Mmmm-hmmmm! I do I do I do I *doo-ooh!"* sang Kel. He then grabbed a bottle opener and popped the top of the orange soda bottle. Much to his surprise, however, the bottle cap came off with such force that it flew into the air, headed for the counter, and landed directly in the hole of the turkey. "Uh-oh," said Kel.

Kenan had not noticed what had happened. "Uh-oh, what?"

"My bottle cap flew into the turkey," explained Kel.

"What?" squealed a suddenly horrified Kenan.

"Don't worry," said Kel. "I'll get it." He stuck his hand deep inside the opening of the turkey. "I can feel it . . . yeah I almost got it. . . . Wait, wait! There it is . . . oww!" screamed Kel. "It's hot!"

"Then take your hand out of the turkey," suggested Kenan.

"I can't!" replied Kel, in obvious pain. "It's stuck!" His hand stuck inside the still hot turkey, Kel started to panic. He began wildly swinging the arm with the turkey attached, but it was no use. The bird would not come loose. Kenan was barely able to get out of the way of Kel's wild swings, as Kel broke practically every single item in the kitchen in an attempt to free his hand of the boiling bird.

"Aw, this can't be happening to me!" cried Kenan.

Kel tried banging the turkey as hard as he could on the kitchen table, knocking everything off of it, and eventually knocking over the whole kitchen table. Kenan frantically tried to calm Kel down, while attempting to pull the turkey off his hand, but Kel, hysterical with pain, ran screaming into the living room, where Kyra and the guests were still waiting for dinner. Of course, Kenan followed him.

Now in the living room, Kel turned in circles, trying to fling the piping hot turkey off his hand, and breaking everything in his way. Kyra and the relatives were horrified. Aunt Gerdie got up from her chair. "Is that a *turkey* on that boy's hand?" she asked in a high-pitched tone.

Screaming and swinging his arm wildly over the couch Kel knocked Grandma Molly in the head with the turkey, sending her flying to the floor, still snoring away.

"Grandma Molly!" shouted Aunt Gerdie.

"Yaagghhhh!" screamed Kel.

While Kenan grabbed Kel's hand to try to pull the turkey off, Uncle Raymond seized the opportunity and snatched a tiny piece off of it. After all, he was awfully hungry and he'd been waiting a long time.

"Stop eating the turkey!" said Kenan to Uncle Raymond.

Kel just couldn't hold still long enough for Kenan to remove the turkey from his hand. Overcome with pain, Kel ran face first into the closet door.

Meanwhile, Tootie and Regine, the two live turkeys who'd made their way upstairs unseen by all, were now on their way down the stairs to see what all the commotion was about.

It was a disaster.

And just to make it a little worse, Roger and Sheryl arrived. They opened the front door to absolute mayhem. Two live turkeys walked directly past them. Kel was running around their living room with a cooked turkey stuck to his hand, breaking their furniture. Kenan was chasing Kel, trying to remove the turkey from his hand, while Uncle Raymond was trying to eat the turkey. Finally, Kenan managed to catch Kel and hold him down on the sofa. Kenan began to pull as hard as he could on the turkey.

Sheryl and Roger stood at the front door in shock. "What are you guys doing with my bird?" screamed Roger. Coincidentally, it was at that precise moment that Kenan finally freed the turkey from Kel's hand. Unfortunately, however, Kenan yanked so hard that the turkey went flying from Kel's hand, all the way across the living room, and right into Roger's face, making a loud *smack!* Roger fell flat on his back. Tootie and Regine gobbled loudly as Sheryl and Kyra bent over to check on Roger.

This Thanksgiving was, without a doubt, the worst Thanksgiving ever. "Kel?" said Kenan.

"Huh?" replied Kel.

"Which way are you gonna run?"

"That way," said Kel, pointing that way.

"Cool. I'll go this way," said Kenan, pointing this way.

Kenan and Kel ran in opposite directions, as fast as they could.

'TIS THE SEASON TO BE IN TROUBLE

Kenan and Kel come back out through the red curtain with Kel's turkey friend, James. They look themselves over and exchange glances of disbelief. "We're still alive!" shouts Kel, who celebrates by doing a little dance.

"Yeah, I can't believe it," adds Kenan. "I thought for sure my daddy would kill us both." Kenan stops and glares at Kel. "Well, that certainly was an interesting Thanksgiving." Kenan is actually waiting for an apology, here. After all, the tragedy was all Kel's fault.

"Well, I had fun," says Kel.

Kenan can't believe his ears. He thinks about it for a moment. Nope. There was absolutely no way the word *fun* could be used to describe that Thanksgiving. "Fun?" shouts Kenan. "We ruined three turkeys, two ovens, Chris's Thanksgiving dinner, our Thanksgiving dinner, a whole bunch of dishes, and I'm grounded 'til next Thanksgiving."

Turkeys Tootie and Regine now walk out onto the stage. James jumps out of Kel's arms and joins them in a turkey celebration. "Well," says Kel, "at least James has a couple of new friends."

"Yeah, but they're not out of the woods yet," warned Kenan.

"What do you mean?" asks Kel.

"Well, last I heard, people eat turkey for Christmas, too."

Kel immediately runs to his turkey friends and guards them with his body. "Kenan, we gotta protect 'em from all the hungry people! They're my friends!" cries Kel.

"Don't worry," says Kenan. "They'll be safe here until after the holidays."

"Thank you, Kenan. You're our hero," says Kel with sincere appreciation.

"Well, Kel, I guess I can think of *one* good thing that came out of our little Thanksgiving adventure," says Kenan, as he reaches behind the curtain and pulls out two cooked turkeys. "You gave me a great idea when you had your hand stuck in that turkey."

"I did?" asks Kel.

"Yeah, check it out," says Kenan. "Turkey boxing gloves!" Kenan puts a turkey on each hand and pretends to box.

"Hey, that *is* a good idea," Kel observes. "And when you're done boxing, you can eat 'em!"

The turkeys don't take kindly to Kel's suggestion, and gobble loudly in protest.

"I'm sorry, turkey pals!" cries Kel. "I promise I'll never eat turkey again."

Kenan shakes his head at Kel. "Yeah. Like you'll never eat turkey again. Why would you lie like that to the poor, unsuspecting birds?"

"Shhh! I'm still gonna eat lots of turkey, but my turkey friends don't have to know," whispers Kel.

"Okay, Soup Spoon, your secret's safe with me," assures Kenan. "Now, let's go find someone for you to turkey box."

"Kenan, I decided I don't want to turkey box. I'm a lover, not a fighter. I just want to spread joy throughout the world."

"Are you sure you mean joy and not misery?" asks Kenan.

Kel reaches behind the curtain and pulls out two floppy red Santa hats. He takes off his Pilgrim's hat and replaces it with a Santa's hat. Then, he puts the other Santa hat on Kenan's head. He then grabs a handful of fake snow and throws it all over Kenan, and all over the stage.

"Man, what *are* you doing?" asks an annoyed Kenan.

"Where's your Christmas spirit, Kenan?" asks Kel. "Now that Thanksgiving's over, it's officially Christmastime. It's time for givin' and lovin'. It's the time of year to spread good tighties and great joy to each and everyone."

"Good 'tighties'?"

"Uh-huh," Kel replies. "It's the happiest time of

year. It's the time of year where people put up trees and decorate 'em with cans of orange soda, and . . ."

Kenan interrupts. "Tidings."

"What?"

"It's the time of year to spread good *tidings* and great joy," corrects Kenan. "Not 'tighties.'"

"Are you sure?" asks Kel.

"Positive."

"What's a tiding?"

"Uh, well it's uh . . ." Kenan has to think a moment. "Well, it's sort of like a . . . hold on, I'll remember. It's . . ." He realizes he really doesn't know, and becomes rather frustrated. "Well, *iguana,* you're so smart, what's a 'tighty'?"

"Something you spread during the holididdie-ay season," replies Kel confidently.

"Okay, you win," surrenders Kenan. "I'm just now realizing you can't argue with the President of Confusion."

"Princess of Confusion," corrects Kel.

"Oh, yeah. Well, Merry Christmas, Your Highness."

"So, what are ya gonna get me for Christmas, Kenan?"

"I don't know!" snaps Kenan. "It's a whole month away."

"You know, the day after Thanksgiving is the busiest shopping day of the year," Kel reminds Kenan. "I already got your momma and daddy their presents."

Kenan is touched. He hasn't even begun to think about what he was going to get Kel, not to mention his parents. "Really?" says Kenan, his Santa hat flopping straight back. "Well, that's real nice of you, Kel. What did you get them?"

Kel reaches behind the curtain and pulls out a couple of unwrapped boxes. "I can't wait to show you," giggles Kel, as he opens one of the boxes and pulls out a long-haired blond wig. "I got your daddy this wig!" says Kel proudly. "Isn't it beautiful? I figured since your daddy doesn't have any hair of his own, he could really use all this pretty hair."

Kenan just stands there, his eyes and mouth wide open.

"See," continues Kel holding up a comb, "I also got him this comb, so he can style it any way he wants. Don'tcha think it's a great present?"

"He'll love it," says Kenan sarcastically.

Kel reaches into the other box and pulls out a raccoon skin hat, like the kind Davy Crockett used to wear. "And I got this for your momma," brags Kel.

"What is it?"

"It's a raccoon hat." Kel suddenly begins to whisper. "Of course, it's not real raccoon skin. I didn't wanna hurt any cute little raccoon animals."

"That was very humanitarian of you," replies Kenan.

"I know," says Kel. "Your mom will love it."

"I didn't even know she wanted one," says Kenan, somewhat in shock.

"Oh, she never actually told me she wanted one," says Kel. "But it's perfect for those cold winter afternoons, when she's out in the woods huntin' quail and pheasant.''

Kenan is silent as he tries to picture Sheryl Rockmore out in the woods on a snowy afternoon, wearing her imitation raccoon skin hat, hunting quail and pheasant. Completely unable to picture this, Kenan finally breaks the silence. ''Well, I'm sure she'll use it in the best of health.''

''Good!'' says Kel, jubilantly. He then looks at the turkeys who are still milling about on the stage. ''Kenan, I didn't get anything for the turkeys.''

''Don't worry, Kel. You still have a month. Well, I'd love to stay here and hang out with ya, but we have some more stories to tell, and—''

''Kenan, let's tell Christmas stories.''

''Well, that's what we're about to do,'' says Kenan. ''We're going to tell the people a Christmas story.''

''Like that one by that person . . . what was her name? . . . Oh yeah, Christmas Carol, she called herself.''

'' 'Christmas Carol'?'' questions Kenan.

''Yeah, you know,'' continues Kel. ''The one about that dude, Eddie Sneezer Stooge. He's real mean to this guy, Bob Scratchy, who works for him, and . . .''

Oh no, thinks Kenan to himself. *Here it comes . . .*

''. . . and he makes Bob Scratchy work on Christmas Eve, and Bob Scratchy has this kid, Tina Turner—''

''You mean, Tiny Tim?'' asks Kenan, rolling his eyes.

''Yeah, that's her,'' says Kel, not missing a beat. ''. . . anyway, she's got a sore leg, and his family's real

44

poor, and Eddie Sneezer Stooge is real rich, and he gets visited by these three ghosts on Christmas Eve. Let's see . . ." Kel thinks hard while Kenan cringes. ". . . the ghost of Christmas cards, the ghost of Christmas presents, and the ghost of Christmas on other planets. He was the real mean one, as I recall."

"Well," says Kenan, struggling to get the confused Kel off the subject, "I was thinking more along the lines of telling the people one of *our own* Christmas stories."

"Oh!" Kel is excited. "Like the time I shorted out your Christmas tree and set your house on fire?"

"No. I don't think we should tell the people about *that* time."

"How about the Christmas I accidentally stabbed your daddy in the behind with a reindeer?"

"Naw. My dad's rear end starts hurtin' every time someone reminds him of that Christmas. I was thinking we'd tell a whole different kind of story this time."

"A whole different kind? Like what?" asks Kel.

Kenan starts to walk off stage. "We're gonna tell 'em a story about the true meaning of Christmas. Yep. That's what we're gonna do." Kenan then walks off the stage, leaving Kel standing there alone with his thoughts and his turkeys.

"Kenan!" Kel calls out after him. "Whaddaya mean 'the true meaning of Christmas'? Kenan? Am I gonna be haunted by the ghost of after-Christmas sales? Kenan, I'm scared!" Kel turns toward the empty seats. "Aw, here goes Christmas!" he shouts, and runs off after Kenan.

"MERRY CHRISTMAS, KENAN!"

Here's some more candy canes," said Sheryl Rockmore, as she gave a handful of them to her daughter, Kyra. It was Christmastime, the most festive time of year, and the Rockmores were in their living room, decorating their tree. The living room was filled with happy people, decorations, and Christmas spirit. As a matter of fact, the only thing missing from the Rockmore living room was Kenan. It was unlike him not to take part in decorating the Christmas tree, but at that moment, he just wasn't there. Unfortunately for Roger Rockmore, Kel *was* there, in his backward baseball cap, hanging cans of orange soda on the Rockmores' Christmas tree.

"Uh . . . excuse me . . . Kel?" said Roger. "What are you doing?"

"I'm hanging Christmas tree ornaments," replied Kel happily.

"You're hanging up cans of orange soda?" asked

46

Sheryl, somewhat surprised at Kel's rather strange taste in Yuletide decorations.

"Mmmm-hmmmm!" Kel replied. And then he began to sing. *"We wish you an orrr-range Christmas, we wish you an orrr-range Christmas! . . ."*

"And I *wish* you'd go home," said Roger, quite sincerely.

Kel just laughed and slapped Roger on the back. Deep down, Kenan's dad must really like Kel. After all, if he didn't, then why would he allow Kenan to have him over all the time? But if one didn't know better, one might think Kel really got on Roger's nerves.

Kel took his orange soda ornament from the living room into the kitchen, where he finally found his pal Kenan at the kitchen table, completely absorbed in a bicycle catalog.

"Hey, Kenan. Did ya see these?" asked Kel, displaying his lovely can of orange soda. "See my orange soda can ornaments?"

But Kenan was not paying attention. He was into his bike catalog. "Mmm-hmm," he replied without even looking up. "Very orangey."

Frustrated, Kel grabbed the catalog. "What is this?"

"Hey!" yelled Kenan. "Give that back!"

Kel wanted to see what Kenan was so interested in that he couldn't even admire his orange soda can Christmas ornaments. "Oooh!" exclaimed Kel, looking at a picture in the catalog. "A mountain bike!"

"Not just *any* mountain bike," said Kenan, taking the

brochure back from Kel. "That is the Road Blazer Deluxe Elite mountain bike!"

"This bike has everything!" said Kel.

"Yep. Spin wheels, rock shocks, x-ray grip shift, swivel-nut steering, nard guard, titanium frame . . . and it's gonna be my Christmas present!" bragged Kenan.

When Kel asked Kenan who could possibly afford to buy him a Christmas present that expensive, he was rather surprised at Kenan's response.

"Me," Kenan said with pride as he got up, walked over to the fridge, and began pouring himself a glass of milk.

"You?"

Kenan had wanted this bike for a long time. He'd been saving up all year long. "My allowance, the money my grandparents gave me for my birthday," he told Kel, ". . . and almost all the money I've made working at Rigby's."

Kel was concerned. If Kenan spent all that money on that bike, how would he be able to buy Christmas presents for his family, and most importantly, his *friends?*

Kel hinted at this dilemma to Kenan, but Kenan didn't seem to care. He poured some chocolate syrup into his milk and stirred. "Hmmm . . . you like the bike better in Machine Green or Babbaloo Blue?"

Sheryl hurried into the kitchen and told the boys it was time for the big moment—time to put the star on top of the Christmas tree. Now, putting the star on the family Christmas tree definitely seems like it should be a job reserved for a family member, but as far as Kel was concerned, he *was* a member of the Rockmore family.

"I'll do it!" he said, running back into the living room with Kenan and his mom right behind him. *"I'll* put the star up!"

Roger didn't think this was a good idea. "Naw, no, no, no!" he bellowed. "I always put the star up on the tree! That's *my* job. Now, everybody out of the way!" Roger moved quickly toward the tree, trying to get there ahead of Kel, but it was too late. Kel had already taken the star, climbed on a stool, and was beginning to place it on top of the tree. As Kel tried to reach the top of the rather tall tree, however, he knocked the entire tree over.

"Auuughhh!" screamed Roger as the brightly decorated, pointy Christmas tree came crashing down right on top of him, knocking him to the living room floor.

The other Rockmores were silent, their hands over their mouths. Kel stood there on the stool, wincing in fear, as Roger slowly got to his feet. Kyra and Sheryl tried to refrain from laughing because the star that was to be placed on top of the tree was now stuck to the top of Roger's head. He was fuming.

"Well, bye!" said Kel abruptly, and he ran quickly toward the front door, grabbed his coat, and raced out, just out of the reach of Roger, who chased him out the door.

Rigby's Grocery Store was decorated all over with gold tinsel and brightly colored Christmas lights. Kenan handed Mrs. Quagmeyer her bag of groceries, then leaned against the counter in his blue Rigby's apron.

"Okay, Mrs. Quagmeyer. There ya go. Merry Christmas," said Kenan coldly.

Mrs. Quagmeyer was full of the Christmas spirit. "Oh, thank you, young man! I do love Christmas!"

Kenan wasn't interested. He just wanted Mrs. Quagmeyer to leave. "I bet you do," said Kenan, hoping that would be the end of the conversation.

"And I love to sing Christmas carols!" added Mrs. Quagmeyer.

"Okay. Bye-bye now," said Kenan, waving.

Mrs. Quagmeyer was a nice old lady and a regular customer at Rigby's, but today, Kenan just wasn't interested in anything she had to say about Christmas.

"Would you like to hear a Christmas carol?" asked Mrs. Quagmeyer enthusiastically.

"No, no. I'm allergic," replied Kenan.

But Mrs. Quagmeyer paid no attention, and began loudly singing "The Twelve Days of Christmas." *"On the first day of Christmas, my true love gave to me . . ."*

"Aw, man . . . ," complained Kenan. She was really beginning to annoy him. Could it be possible? Annoy him with a *Christmas carol?* What was the matter with Kenan, anyway? For some reason, he just didn't seem to have any Christmas spirit this year.

". . . a partridge in a pear tree!" continued Mrs. Quagmeyer. She moved her gloved hands back and forth as if she were conducting her own orchestra.

"Thank you!" cried Kenan, as if he were in pain. "Have a nice—"

Mrs. Quagmeyer simply continued singing louder, and with more gusto. *"On the second day of Christmas, my true love gave to me . . ."*

"Whyyyyyy?" shouted Kenan, completely exasperated.

". . . two turtle doves, and a partridge in a pear tree! On the . . ."

Kenan had to think fast. "Twelfth!" he shouted out.

". . . twelfth day of Christmas my true love gave to me . . . ," sang Mrs. Quagmeyer. It worked. Kenan had somehow propelled her all the way to the last verse of the song. He quickly rushed out from behind the counter and gently escorted Mrs. Quagmeyer out of the store, while singing his own version of the song at a very fast pace.

". . . Twelve loads of luggage, ten funky chickens, nine lumps of liver, seven pimples poppin', six ladies' dresses, four rotten pumpkins, two Caesar salads, and a park bench in a prune tree! Bye!"

"Bye!" said a confused Mrs. Quagmeyer, just before Kenan slammed the door in her face. Kenan was finally rid of that crazy singing madwoman. He breathed a sigh of relief as he made his way back toward the counter, where he picked up his bicycle catalog. That was all he seemed to care about these days. He knew he was becoming obsessed with that mountain bike.

"Hey, Kenan, look what I got!" shouted Chris. Chris

Potter, in his gray Rigby's manager's apron, wheeled a mechanical Santa Claus in from the back room. "It's a life-size mechanical Santa Claus! Look at it!"

Kenan thought it looked a little *too* lifelike. In fact, he thought it was kind of scary-looking. "Oooh. Where'd you get that, Chris?"

"I found it out back in the garbage," he replied. Chris was excited about his find. It looked just like the real Santa Claus, except maybe a little shorter. It had on the traditional red suit, floppy red hat, and black belt, and it had a fluffy white beard and mustache. Chris struggled to get the heavy mechanical Santa to stand upright. "Whoa, he's heavy! Come help me set him up, Kenan!"

Again, Kenan was completely uninterested. All he wanted to do was go in the back room and stare at the picture of his mountain bike in that catalog. "Oooh, I would," said Kenan in his most insincere tone, "but it's my break." He took his catalog and headed for the back room, leaving Chris to struggle with the heavy robot Santa.

"Oh, *fine,*" said Chris, hurt and annoyed. "I'll do it myself."

Kenan walked into the dull-looking back room of Rigby's, where he could swear he heard someone singing "Jingle Bells." He walked past the shelves, filing cabinets and boxes, the refrigerator and break table, all the way to the back door. There, out in the alley, were Kel and Mrs. Quagmeyer, bundled up in heavy coats in the cold Chicago night, happily singing "Jingle Bells" while warming themselves over a small trash can fire.

"Jingle Bells, jingle bells, jingle all the way!" they sang. *"Oh what fun it is to ride in a one horse open . . ."*

Kenan was irritated. "Kel!" he interrupted, angrily. "Would you get in here!" Kenan grabbed Kel, yanked him inside, and, once again, shut the door on poor Mrs. Quagmeyer in mid-carol. It didn't matter to her. She just kept singing.

"What are you doing in the alley?" Kenan demanded.

"Singing with the elderly," replied Kel, spotting the bicycle catalog in Kenan's hand. "Man, you're still staring at that mountain bike?"

Kenan couldn't help it. All Christmas meant to him this year was that mountain bike. He cared about nothing else.

"Kenan! Come give me a hand with this mechanical Santa!" yelled Chris from inside the store.

Kenan was annoyed. He didn't care to be bothered with helping Chris. "What? . . ." he yelled back in a grouchy tone.

Back in the store, Chris continued to struggle with robot Santa. He had him propped upright, but he couldn't get the plug to reach into the wall. He called out to Kenan. "Come help me plug this thing in!"

"I'm on my break!" shouted Kenan from the back room.

"Oh, I have to do everything myself," complained

Chris to himself. Chris bent over, and, holding onto the Santa with one hand, he finally managed to reach the wall outlet with the other and plug in the mechanical Santa. Suddenly, the sound of an old motor whirring could be heard from inside Santa's stomach. Slowly and mechanically, the Santa began to move his arms. Chris smiled. *I did it!* The thing actually worked. He reached over to touch the Santa on the shoulder, when a strange thing happened. The mechanical Santa grabbed Chris by the shoulders and began shaking him back and forth, then wrestled him to the ground.

"Hey!" yelled Chris. "What the? . . ."

The Santa then pinned Chris, sat on top of him, and began slapping him on either side of his face with each of his white gloved hands.

"Kenan!" screamed Chris, on his back on Rigby's floor, helpless against the mechanical Santa. "Kenan!" But it was to no avail. Kenan only cared about one thing, and it wasn't whether or not Chris got beaten up by Santa. Chris continued to struggle, his floppy dark brown hair falling in front of his eyes, as the robot Santa flailed on top of him. "Get off me!" he yelled. "Stop it! Get off me!" It was at that moment that two small boys happened into Rigby's.

"Hey! Santa's pinned that guy!" yelled one of the boys.

"Coooool!" said the other boy.

Excited to see this one-sided wrestling match, they rushed over to get a closer look.

"Come on, Santa! Go, Santa!" they shouted. "Get 'im, Santa!"

In the back room, Kenan continued to ignore Chris's screams for help. Instead, he had an idea. "Hey, Kel. Come with me to the mall and see my bike."

"What about the store?" asked Kel.

"Aw, Chris can handle it 'til I get back," said Kenan as he removed his apron. "Come on!"

They grabbed their coats and headed out the back door into the alley, where Mrs. Quagmeyer was still standing over the fire, singing happily away, but in a much more jazzy tempo. *"In a one horse open sleigh, over fields we go . . ."*

". . . Laughing all the way. Ha ha ha!" sang Kel, snapping his fingers. Kenan, still annoyed, shook his head in disgust, as he and Kel walked away.

Like all department stores at Christmastime, Putman's was decorated from floor to ceiling. Christmas music was being piped in on the store sound system, and there were many shoppers frantically searching for presents. Kenan and Kel were in the bicycle section, gazing in awe at the mountain bike that Kenan loved so much. And a beautiful bike it was. It seemed to shine brighter than any of the other bikes, and it appeared to have on it every contraption known to man.

"There she is!" exclaimed Kenan. "The bike of bikes. What do you think?"

Kel was overwhelmed. "I have never wanted to sit upon something so badly."

The salesman was wearing a dark three-piece suit with a Christmassy red-and-green plaid vest. He walked over to Kenan and Kel, looking to make a big sale. He recognized Kenan immediately. "Well, look who's back again," he said. "Shall I wrap it up and pop a bow on it?"

Kenan assured him that he almost had enough money saved up and would buy the bike very soon. The salesman knew he had Kenan hooked. And, being a good salesman, he reminded Kenan that if he didn't buy the bike now, it might not be there much longer.

"Christmas is only three days away. I hope nobody snatches it up," said the crafty salesman, as he began to walk away.

Kenan squealed at the very idea of missing out on an opportunity to get that bike.

"Wait!" Kel called out. "Can't you hold it for him until he gets all the money?"

"I'm sorry," said the salesman, sounding like he really wasn't that sorry. "No can do."

That was it. Kenan hastily reached into his pocket and pulled out some cold, hard cash. "Well, what if I put down a hundred dollars?" he asked, handing the money to the pleasantly surprised salesman.

"Yes!" he sang. "*Can* do! I'll go ring you up a hold slip. Back in a moochie!"

Kenan and Kel exchanged peculiar glances. " 'Moochie'?'' they said in unison, as the salesman scurried off.

Kenan leaned over his prize dark green mountain bike and stroked its soft vinyl seat. He even spoke to the bike. "Ooh, don't worry, baby," said Kenan to the bicycle. "Soon, I'll get you out of here and take you home where I can give you the lovin' you deserve."

Kel suggested that Kenan climb on the bike.

"Do I dare?" asked Kenan.

"I think you do," replied Kel.

Kenan glanced around to make sure no one was looking, then gently climbed up on the bike and made himself comfortable. Then, he actually grabbed the handlebars. Kenan was in ecstasy!

"How does it feel?" asked Kel.

"Wow! It's . . . it's hard to describe," began Kenan, smiling widely. "I feel all tingly and warm and all squishy inside."

Unbeknownst to Kenan and Kel, the salesman had returned and was standing right there. "Uh, excuse the news," he said, "but until you pay for that in full, there will be no sitting or touching."

"Oh, sorry," said Kenan. Kenan then tried to get off the bike, but he simply couldn't. He was so in love with it that, somehow, his body wouldn't let him. Finally, Kel had to physically help Kenan off the bike.

"Sorry," apologized Kel to the salesman. "He's a little emotional."

"I do not judge," said the salesman. He then handed

Kenan the hold slip and a pen and promised him they would hold the bike for him until Christmas Eve. Kenan signed the slip and handed it back to the salesman, who checked it over carefully. "Perfect," said the salesman. "Hasta la see ya!"

Again, Kenan and Kel exchanged peculiar glances.

"'Hasta la see ya'?" they said in unison as the salesman walked away. This salesmen was using words that Kenan and Kel had simply never heard before.

Kel suggested that they'd better leave before Kenan started to drool over the bike and rust it. Kenan agreed, and they went to check out the toy department.

Kenan and Kel, surrounded by kids, were browsing through the toy department when Kel noticed something cool. He might as well still have been six years old the way he rushed over and picked up a large blue toy tuba. "It's a Tuba-Phone!" he exclaimed. Kenan just shrugged, never having heard of one of those. "It's not just a tuba," Kel explained, reaching into the tuba and pulling out a telephone. "It's also a phone! Is that cool or what?"

"Oh, *yes*," said Kenan. "Many a time I'll be talking on the telephone and thinking to myself, 'You know, if only I could be playing a tuba during this conversation.'"

"Me too!" said Kel with the utmost sincerity.

At Christmastime *every* department store had a department store Santa. Putman's was no different. Just a few feet away from where Kenan and Kel were standing, the Putman's Santa was sitting in his huge chair surrounded by giant candy canes and presents. Behind him was a large cardboard cutout of Santa's house with cardboard cutout Christmas trees, flanked by large toy soldiers. Unlike the mechanical Santa that was still at Rigby's beating the tar out of Chris, this Santa seemed like the real thing. He was a jolly old man with spectacles, a full white beard, and a deep voice.

"Well, ho ho ho!" said Santa to a little boy who had come to sit on his lap. "What's your name, little fella?"

The little boy appeared harmless enough. He was well-dressed in a neat white shirt with a red bow tie and suspenders. "Sam. My name is Sam," he said in a businesslike tone.

"Well, Sam, have you been a good boy this year?" asked Santa.

"Can we just get down to business?" snapped Sam. Santa was a bit taken aback. Most of the children enjoyed a little of the traditional chitchat before the actual gift requests were made. But, evidently, not Sam.

"Uh, sure," replied Santa, nervously. "And what would you like for Christmas?"

"I want an airplane," demanded Sam.

"An airplane?"

"You heard me, fat boy!" replied Sam in a threatening tone. "I want a real Air Force fighter jet."

The department store Santa was wondering what the real Santa would say in that situation. "A real fighter jet? Uh . . . ho ho ho!" he laughed.

Sam was not amused. "What's with the 'ho hos'? Did

I say something funny? Am I some kind of clown? I said I want a plane!" shouted Sam.

Santa was now extremely uneasy. "But that's much too big a present for a little boy. Ho ho—"

Wham! Before Santa knew it, Sam belted him with a right cross to the jaw. Santa flew right off his chair and flat on his back. Immediately, kids and their parents surrounded the fallen Santa as the nervous store manager, Mr. Gordon, rushed to the scene.

"What's going on? What's happened?" asked Mr. Gordon, frantically.

A young blond-haired mother responded. "Some tough kid belted Santa!"

Mr. Gordon took a look at his Santa. He was definitely unconscious. Mr. Gordon was beside himself. It was Christmastime, his store was packed with kids, and he was fresh out of Santas. "Oh dear!" he said as he tried to revive Santa. "Santa Claus! Santa, wake up! Please wake up! Oh, good heavens!"

The parents were not pleased. "Hey!" shouted the blond mother. "My kid's been waiting in line for a half hour to see Santy Claus! What are you going to do about it?"

Another angry mom chimed in. "My kid's been waiting an *hour!*"

"I want to see Santy Claus!" shouted the kids. It was a disaster. If Mr. Gordon didn't find another Santa Claus right away, a riot was going to break out in his store.

"All right, all right!" he screamed. "No need to mob up! I'll . . . see what I can do. Please don't destroy my store!" he pleaded. He then rushed off to try to find a replacement Santa. As he milled about through the store, he saw Kenan and Kel, still standing there playing with the Tuba-Phone. "You two!" yelled Mr. Gordon as he approached Kenan and Kel. "I need one of you to be Santa Claus!" Kenan and Kel exchanged their third peculiar glance since walking into Putman's. "Please!" begged Mr. Gordon. "I've got fifty angry parents and children demanding to see Santa Claus!"

Kenan was not sympathetic. "Sorry, man. I can't be Santa Claus."

"Later," said Kel to the wild-eyed Mr. Gordon. Kenan and Kel then started to walk away.

"I'll pay you one hundred dollars!" yelled Mr. Gordon. It was the last act of a desperate man, but it worked. Kenan and Kel stopped dead in their tracks.

"That's almost enough to get you that bike," said Kel.

Kenan wanted that bike more than anything in the world. And even though he had already paid a hundred dollars and had signed the hold slip, he had no idea how he would possibly get the rest of the money by Christmas Eve. Now, there was a way.

Mr. Gordon, meanwhile, was about to have a nervous breakdown. "Well?" he said. "Will you be Santa? What do you say?"

"I say . . . ho ho ho!" laughed Kenan.

Relieved, Mr. Gordon led Kenan and Kel to the dressing room, where Kenan could change into a Santa outfit.

The parents and kids were not happy. They were angrily screaming, "Santa! Santa! Santa!" and soon they were going to become a vicious, destructive mob. Mr. Gordon couldn't hold them back much longer. So, it was perfect timing when Kenan finally emerged in his Santa Claus outfit.

"Hey, it's Santa Claus!" shouted an excited kid. The rest of the kids and parents cheered when Kenan, dressed as Santa, took his seat in the big Santa chair.

"Now, just sit here, and, you know, *be* Santa," instructed the nervous Mr. Gordon, before hurrying off.

"Ho ho ho!" Kenan gave his best Santa laugh.

"And I'm Santa's little elf!" announced Kel, as he ran out wearing a ridiculous-looking red-and-green elf's outfit. Actually, he looked more like a joker from a deck of playing cards than an elf. But somehow, in a strange way, it seemed to fit Kel perfectly.

It seemed easy enough at first. All Kenan had to do was sit in that chair, let little kids sit in his lap and ask for things, and he'd get a hundred dollars and his new mountain bike. The first child, a little boy named Raymond, asked for a Tuba-Phone.

"Yes!" said Kel, who was standing at Santa's side. "Good call!"

"Thanks, elf," said little Raymond.

"Okay, Raymond. Santa will do his best to bring you a Tuba-Phone. Ho ho ho!" replied Kenan.

"Thanks, Santa!" said Raymond, giving him a hug.

"No problem. Stay cool!" said Kenan.

Kel was impressed. "Hey, you're good at this," he whispered to Kenan.

"Yeah," whispered Kenan. "And this is a lot easier than working at Rigby's."

Speaking of Rigby's, unlike Mr. Gordon, Chris had still not solved *his* Santa problem. The mean, mechanical Santa now had Chris pinned facedown on the counter in front of a loud cheering crowd that had gathered inside the store. Santa was pulling hard on Chris's leg with one hand, and pulling hard on his arm with the other hand.

"Santa! Santa! Santa!" cheered the wrestling fans at Rigby's, led, of course, by the ever enthusiastic Mrs. Quagmeyer.

"Kenan! Where are you?" screamed Chris, as the robot Santa continued to torture him.

It was getting late, and Kenan had made promises to almost every kid in Putman's Department Store.

"Next!" he called out, beginning to enjoy his new job.

A sweet little European girl in an old-fashioned green-and-red dress and a pretty black hat approached Santa with her mother. "Santa Claus, this is Keeshka," said

Keeshka's mom. "She is from Feeshlakia and I'm afraid she doesn't speak any English. I told her you wouldn't be able to talk to her because you are probably not the real Santa Claus."

Kenan couldn't allow Keeshka to know that he wasn't the real Santa Claus. It would break her heart. He looked at Keeshka, and began speaking what he hoped would sound like Feeshlakian. "Keeshka! Ingen shmeegngin doogin wirshka?" asked Kenan.

Keeshka's eyes lit up with joy. "Ooh, Shanta Klooz!" said Keeshka, running to sit on Kenan's lap. "Arbin shmarbin wirshka dooba!"

"Oogin loomin veemin shlooger?" asked Kenan.

Kel could not believe this. He was in a daze. How was Kenan able to speak Feeshlakian so well?

"Neeks!" said Keeshka. "Deenga spoogin loomin poo!"

"Neeks!" shouted Kenan. "Spoona pina loomin singa?"

Keeshka nodded. "Neeks! Neeks!" she said with glee.

Then, all at once, Kenan and Keeshka began singing "Jingle Bells" together in her own weird Feeshlakian language. *"Shlingin poon, Shlingin poon . . . irshka dirshka doo! Leeman poo, oon vleemin doo, da ishka mishka slay!"*

Kenan "Ho ho hod" one more time, and Keeshka hugged him as hard as she could. "Ooh, schminga beesh, do Shanta Klooz!"

"Hey, you're welcome," said Kenan. "Merry Christmas!"

"Neeks!" said Kel the elf, waving good-bye, as Keeshka and her mother walked away.

There were only two kids left waiting to see Santa Claus. It was a tiny little girl and her older brother, who must have been about eight. "Just wait here, okay Katie?" instructed the boy. His little sister nodded, and he went to sit on Santa's lap.

"A-ho ho ho!" said Kenan. "What's your name, little boy?"

"I'm Daniel Miller," he said. "It's nice to meet you, Santa. Over there's my little sister, Katie." Daniel pointed to his timid little sister. She was adorable, with straight gold bangs almost covering her big sad blue eyes. *She can't be more than five years old,* Kenan thought, remembering how cute his own little sister used to be. Before she turned into a brat.

"Hi there, Katie!" shouted Kenan. He then turned back to Daniel. "And what can Santa bring you for Christmas this year?" he asked in his best, deepest Santa voice.

"Oh, nothing for me, thanks," replied Daniel, graciously.

Kenan was so thunderstruck that he accidentally lost his Santa voice for a moment. "Whaddaya mean, 'nothing'?" he demanded. Kenan had absolutely no idea where young Daniel was coming from. He couldn't imagine not wanting something for Christmas. He

65

couldn't stop thinking about how badly he wanted that mountain bike. Surely, Daniel must have yearned for *something*.

"I was just hoping that maybe you could bring my little sister Katie a new bicycle," explained Daniel. "She'd ask you herself, but she's kind of shy."

"Yes, but what do *you* want for Christmas?" Kenan persisted.

"Oh, don't worry about me," said Daniel. "Just a new bike for my little sister. See . . . ," he explained, ". . . she had a bike, but it got stolen, and my mom can't afford to get her a new one."

Kenan was touched. He was more than touched. He felt like a complete fool. "Oh, well . . ." he said, his voice starting to break with emotion, "Santa will do his best to bring your little sister a new bike this Christmas."

Daniel was excited. "You mean it? Wow! Thanks Santa!" He jumped off Kenan's lap and turned to his sister. "Katie! Santa's gonna bring you a new bike! Come say thanks!"

Cute little Katie walked slowly over to Kenan in her tattered red coat, gave him a big hug, and quickly ran off.

"She's just shy," explained Daniel. "Thanks for everything, Santa!" With that, Daniel ran to catch up with his sister.

A pretty woman dressed in an old gray coat over an old, ragged dress approached Kenan and Kel. "Hi, I'm their mother," she said. "Thank you for being so nice to my little boy and girl."

Kenan looked up at her with hope in his eyes. "So, uh . . . Mrs. Miller? You're going to get her a new bike for Christmas?"

"I wish I could," she said, "but I just can't afford it. Don't worry. I'll find a way to explain it to them. I'll just tell them Santa got lost or something."

Kenan and Kel gulped, as if they were trying to swallow something big and painful.

"They'll understand," she continued. "Bye, now. And Merry Christmas." Mrs. Miller went off to catch up with her kids.

"Merry Christmas," said Kenan and Kel. Kenan and Kel looked at each other sadly. "Um . . . Merry Christmas," they said to each other, without any heart.

Rigby's had finally quieted down. The robot Santa was sitting, handcuffed against the wall, with a sign around his neck that read DANGER. Chris was at the hospital having X rays. Kenan and Kel, back in their regular clothes, stood at the counter, drinking glasses of orange soda.

"Man, you sure were a great Santa Claus," said Kel.

But Kenan didn't even want to think about it. Something was bothering him. "You know, you should play Santa Claus all year round," continued Kel.

"Would you stop with that, already?" snapped Kenan.

"What's wrong?"

"I can't stop thinking about that family," said Kenan sadly. "That poor little bikeless girl."

It was right then that Chris walked in. His arm was in a sling, and he had two black eyes. "Kenan, I'm back," he announced, then flinched and let out a little yelp when he walked by the mechanical Santa. "I have your paycheck," he informed Kenan, handing him an envelope.

Kel knew immediately what this meant. "Ooh! Kenan! Now you got enough money to go get your mountain bike!"

"Oh, yeah!" said Kenan, suddenly excited.

Kel told Kenan he'd better hurry and get back to Putman's before it closed. So, off Kenan went. In a few minutes, all the waiting would be over, and the Road Blazer Deluxe Elite would be all his.

Back at Putman's Department Store, the salesman was spraying the bikes with a cleaner and wiping them down. "Well, well!" he said, upon seeing Kenan again. "I was wondering if you were going to be a no-show or a show-show." It was another one of his new words, but Kel wasn't there to share a peculiar glance with.

"I'm a 'show-show,'" replied Kenan. He couldn't wait to get his hands on his new bike. He reached down to touch the seat. "Ohhh . . . ," said Kenan, as he ran his hand across the bike.

"So, did you bring el-money-o?" asked the salesman, as he moved Kenan's hand away from the bike.

"Yeah," replied Kenan, staring in awe at the possession of his dreams. He reached into his pocket and pulled out a big wad of bills—his pay from Mr. Gordon and Rigby's. "I got it all right here." Just as Kenan was about to hand the salesman the money, he heard a distinctive sound. It was the sound of a little bell—the kind one finds on a little kid's bike. Kenan glanced over to see a little girl sitting on a new bike that her dad had just bought for her. She was happily ringing the bell. It reminded Kenan of little Katie. Suddenly, he could feel his heart drop right into his stomach.

"Well," said the aggressive salesman. "Should I ring her up?" There was no response. Kenan just stared at the little girl and her dad. "Knock knock!" shouted the salesman, trying to regain Kenan's attention.

Kenan looked at the beautiful mountain bike that he wanted so badly. He looked at all the money he had in his hand, then over at the row of little girls' bikes.

"We're not getting any younger," reminded the salesman. "Do you want the mountain bike? Yay or nay?"

Kenan just stood there and thought.

It was late on a cold, snowy Christmas Eve. Kenan, dressed in his Santa's outfit from Putman's Department Store, peered through the frosty window of the Millers' living room. He then opened the window and quietly climbed in, just before accidentally closing the window on his hand. "Ow!"

He carried a sack of toys as he searched through the

little house. "Now, where's the tree?" he asked himself as he searched. Finally, he found it. It was a tiny little tree, with just a few cheap decorations. Kenan was moved. "Oh, what a cute little tree!" he whispered to himself.

It was then that Mrs. Miller peeked around from the dark hallway in her nightgown. Frightened that Kenan might be a burglar, she grabbed a heavy toy soldier from a table and sneaked up behind Kenan. She was just about to conk him over the head with it, when Kenan turned around. They stared at each other, and they both screamed at the top of their lungs.

"I'm sorry! I'm sorry!" said Kenan, catching his breath.

"Aren't you the Santa Claus from Putman's Department Store?" asked Mrs. Miller, catching her breath.

"Yeah, uh, that would be me," replied Kenan.

"What are you doing here?"

Kenan was nervous. He figured he was in big trouble. "Well, see . . . I was just . . ."

Daniel and little Katie, having been awakened by all the commotion, ran into the living room in their pajamas, holding hands.

"Santa Claus!" shouted Daniel. He and his sister ran over to Kenan.

"Merry Christmas, Daniel! Merry Christmas, Katie!"

"What are you doing here?" asked Daniel.

"Whaddaya think I'm doing here?" asked Kenan, accidentally using his normal Kenan voice instead of his deep Santa voice. He caught himself, and immediately got back in character. "I mean, I've brought you presents! Ho ho ho!"

With that, Kenan dumped the contents of his sack onto the Millers' living room floor. Daniel and Katie's eyes lit up at the sight of the gift-wrapped presents. They raced to open them up.

Mrs. Miller was about to cry. She knew Kenan wasn't the real Santa Claus, and that could only have meant that he had spent his own money for these gifts for her kids. "This is very nice of you . . . 'Santa.'"

"Ohh," said Kenan, blushing. "Ho ho ho!"

"Whoa!" yelled Daniel, after opening his present. "A portable CD player!"

Katie pulled a huge stuffed bunny out of her box. She smiled and hugged it tightly. Mrs. Miller told them to go back to bed, and they'd open the rest of their presents in the morning.

"Yes, kids," said Kenan. "Santa must be on his way." He began walking toward the door, and then he stopped. "But before I go . . ." Kenan opened the Millers' front door, stepped outside for a moment, and then returned wheeling in the cutest little girl's bike there ever was. It was pink with a big basket in front, tassels, a horn, and white-wall tires. "Would anyone like one of these?" he asked. Little Katie raised her hand high. She was the happiest kid in Chicago. "Well, then Merry Christmas, Katie!"

"Thank you, Santa Claus!" said Katie, as she hopped up on her new bike.

But Santa was not through. "Oh, and uh . . .

Daniel . . . ," said Kenan. He went back outside the front door and returned a moment later with a brand-new little kid's mountain bike. "Ya like mountain bikes?" asked Kenan.

Daniel was floored. His mouth was practically stuck wide open. "Absolutely!"

"Well?" said Kenan, pointing to the bike, "Then get yourself up on there, son!"

Daniel raced over to his bike and jumped on top of it. Kenan put his arms around him and his sister and ho ho ho'd. It was truly a merry Christmas for Kenan.

The merriest Christmas he ever had.

That Christmas Eve at the Rockmores' was particularly festive. Everyone sat on the couch for dessert after a huge turkey dinner. (Don't worry! It wasn't James, Tootie, or Regine.) Even Chris was there, his arm in a sling and his face still bruised from the attack by the robot Santa.

"All right, then!" said Roger, after they finished their dessert. "Let's get to it!" Kel and the Rockmores jumped up from the couch and headed toward the Christmas tree.

"What are we doing?" asked Chris.

Sheryl explained to Chris that every Christmas Eve, they let each of the kids pick one present to open.

Kel quickly shoved a present in Kenan's hand. "Here, open this one. It's from me," said Kel, beaming with excitement as Kenan opened the box. It was something Kenan never thought he'd ever own—battery-powered underpants. "They keep you toasty warm in the winter," explained Kel.

"That's very thoughtful," said Kenan, who then handed Kel his present. Kel opened it like a starving man opens a bag of potato chips. Yep. It was the Tuba-Phone. Kel was ecstatic.

"What about Kyra?" asked Chris.

"Yes, Kyra," said Sheryl. "It's your turn to pick a present."

"I can pick any one I want?" asked Kyra.

"That's the rule," said Roger.

Kyra's choice was easy. "I pick Kel!" She ran over to him and put her arms around him.

"Kenan! Your little sister's squeezing me again," complained Kel.

"Kyra, if you're picking Kel for your present, you'd better keep the receipt," warned Roger.

Well, it was time for Chris and Kel to go home, and time for the Rockmores to go to bed. The next morning would be Christmas morning, and there were still plenty of presents to open, and plenty of Christmassy things left to do. Chris and Kel thanked the Rockmores and headed home, each with a plate full of leftover mashed potatoes. After they left, Sheryl sat down on the couch next to Kenan. "Kenan?" she said. "We know what you did."

Immediately, Kenan thought he was in trouble. What did he do? Did he break an expensive appliance? Did he annoy someone his mom knows? "Uh-what are you talking about?" he asked.

"Kel told us about you giving up your mountain bike to buy presents for those poor children," said Sheryl.

"Oh, *that,*" said Kenan, relieved he hadn't broken anything. "That was nothing."

"No, that was *something,*" said Sheryl. "We know how much you wanted that mountain bike."

"We're very proud of you, Kenan," added Roger.

And why shouldn't they be proud? Kenan had done a wonderful thing. He had finally learned the true meaning of Christmas. And he had ended up with two of the best presents of all: the smiles on the faces of Daniel and Katie, and the admiration of his family.

"Well, I figure if I start saving up now, maybe I'll be able to buy that mountain bike next Christmas," said Kenan.

Sheryl leaned over and kissed Kenan, and everyone headed upstairs for bed . . . except Kenan. He stayed behind for just a minute and picked up the bicycle catalog. He stared one last time at the picture of his beloved mountain bike.

"The Road Blazer Deluxe Elite," he said to himself. "The bike of bikes. Maybe next year." With that, Kenan turned out the light and went upstairs to go to bed.

The living room was completely dark now, except for the colorful Christmas lights. All was quiet, except for the sound of someone struggling to get down the Rockmores' chimney. That's right, it was Claus, himself. The real deal. Red suit and all. Santa Claus quietly wheeled in the Road Blazer Deluxe Elite and left it by the Rockmores' tree.

"Ho ho ho!" Santa laughed to himself. Then he picked up his bag of toys and walked back toward the fireplace. "Merry Christmas to all," he whispered, as he started back up the Rockmores' chimney. "And to all, a good night."

HAPPY NEW YEAR, KEL!

Kenan and Kel walk back through the curtain on stage still wearing their red Santa hats. Kel is crying his eyes out. Kenan hands him a handkerchief to blow his nose.

"I'm sorry, Kenan! I just can't help it!" sobs Kel. "That last adventure was just so moving! I think I'm gonna cry all the way to New Year's Day!"

"Please don't," says Kenan. He points to the three turkeys, who are gobbling happily. "Look at your turkey friends, Kel. They read about our last adventure, and you don't see them crying."

"That's because they're grown turkeys. Everyone knows grown turkeys don't cry."

"Well, you're a grown boy—sort of," Kenan reasons. "Take a lesson from the turkeys man, and get a hold of yourself!"

"But, Kenan. That part where you gave that little girl

that bike . . . it was *beautiful,* man!" Kel begins sobbing uncontrollably.

Kenan is now beginning to cry. "I know," says Kenan. "That was pretty darn nice of me, wasn't it?"

"Yeah!" cries Kel. "And then at the end when Santy Claus came to your house and gave you the Road Blazer Deluxe Elite. Man, that fat man is so sweet!"

Kenan has now joined Kel in "full sob." "Yeah, that Santa is one fly dude! I can't believe how nice that was. It touched me, man! It really touched me!"

"Yeah. A good Christmas story always does that to ya," says Kel. "Like, remember that one where that tornado hits and that little girl wants to follow some yellow sick toad back to Kansas City . . ."

Kenan stops crying. Listening to Kel ramble about nothing has brought him back to reality.

". . . and she runs around everywhere, wearing these bright red shoes, and she hangs out with these three total freaks who are all afraid of this wicked witch who drives this battery-operated mop, and they wanna see this lizard who makes all the laws, and—"

Finally, Kenan interrupts. "Kel, what you're trying to describe, I think, is *The Wizard of Oz.*"

"That's it!" yells Kel, so excited that he pushes Kenan over, sending him to the stage floor. The loud thud startles the turkeys and causes them to scramble.

Kenan gets slowly to his feet. *"The Wizard of Oz* is not a Christmas story, *scarecrow!"*

"It's not?" asks Kel. He thinks for a moment. "I always thought it was."

"Forget it," says Kenan. "You're wrong again. Wronger than usual."

"Well, at least I stopped crying."

"That's true," Kenan agrees. "You were gettin' the stage all wet."

"Well, Kenan, I have one more little Christmas surprise for you."

Kenan thinks for a moment. *One more surprise from Kel?* A surprise from Kel could mean complete disaster. "That's okay, Kel. Really. I'm happy with my battery-operated underwear, and my mountain bike, and my mom and dad are happy with their raccoon skin hat and long blond hair, so I think we've had enough surprises this Christmas."

"Just one more thing," says Kel, and he reaches behind the curtain and pulls out Mrs. Quagmeyer, still singing Christmas carols.

"Ohhhhhhhhhhhhhhhhh," Mrs. Quagmeyer sings. *"Deck the halls with boughs of holly! Fa la la la la la la la la!"*

Kenan cringes. Kel reaches back through the curtain, grabs his bright blue Tuba-Phone, and attempts to accompany Mrs. Quagmeyer. Kenan can't help noticing that the frightened turkeys are all running away.

" 'Tis the season to be jolly! Fa la la la la la la la! . . ." Mrs. Quagmeyer continues.

Kenan tries to decide which is more painful—Mrs. Quagmeyer's scratchy voice or Kel's horrible, obnoxious tuba playing.

"Don we now our gay apparel! Fa la la la la la la la!"

"Kel!" shouts Kenan over the noise. "We have to move on to our next adventure!"

"Sing with me this Yuletide carol! Fa la la la la la la la!" croons Mrs. Quagmeyer, relentlessly.

"We're done talkin' about Christmas!" shouts Kenan. "It's time to talk about New Year's, now!"

"Iiiii'm dreaming of a whiiiiite Christmas!" sings Mrs. Quagmeyer.

Desperate to the point of tears, Kenan notices a string hanging from the ceiling. Just to see what happens, he pulls it.

". . . where treetops glisten, and children listen, and sleigh bells—"

Wham! The song is over. The mechanical Santa falls from the ceiling, landing on top of Kel and Mrs. Quagmeyer, knocking them to the ground. Kel gets up and makes sure his tuba isn't damaged. Mrs. Quagmeyer is pinned beneath the robot. Kenan hopes she isn't hurt, and runs over to check on her.

"Are you all right, Mrs. Quagmeyer?"

"No, I'm not all right. This mechanical St. Nick ruined my song!" She gets up and squares off with the robot Santa.

"I'm gonna take you *down,* Santa!" taunts Mrs. Quagmeyer. The two combatants face each other and move around in a circle.

"It seems like a pretty even match," says Kel, "but I'm puttin' my money on the old lady."

"Are you kidding?" says Kenan. "Did you see what that Santa did to Chris? She's going down in the first round."

Mrs. Quagmeyer, wearing her beige overcoat and black scarf, gets the jump on Santa. She gets him in a head lock, and tries to twist his neck. "I've got you now, fatty!" she shouts.

Even the turkeys rush back to watch the exciting bout. Kenan and Kel nod in approval at the action-packed match. It seems like Mrs. Quagmeyer has a decisive edge, but not for long. The mechanical Santa reaches behind and flips her, sending her to the floor. *Wham!* Santa then pins Mrs. Quagmeyer and begins pulling hard on her leg.

"Santa's got her down!" shouts Kenan. "I think she's gonna lose!"

"Sing, Mrs. Quagmeyer! It's your only hope!" yells Kel.

"Rudolf the red-nosed reindeer! . . ." sings Mrs. Quagmeyer, pinned down on the floor by the monster Santa, *". . . had a very shiny nose!"*

It's working. The robot Santa can't handle the horrible noise. He immediately lets go of Mrs. Quagmeyer and puts his robot hands over his ears. Smoke starts pouring from his neck, and he runs around in circles.

". . . and if you ever saw it," continues Mrs. Quagmeyer, *"you might even say it glows!"*

That last verse does the job. The robot Santa overheats and explodes. Sparks fly everywhere. Kel darts over to Mrs. Quagmeyer, and holds her victorious hand in the air.

"I won!" shouts Mrs. Quagmeyer. "I took 'im down, just like I said I would! Did you boys see how I clobbered him? Nobody beats Old Lady Quagmeyer! Come on! Who wants to take me on?" Mrs. Quagmeyer goes back behind the red curtain. Kenan and Kel can still hear her issuing challenges as she makes her way out of the studio. "I'll take anybody down!" she crows, the sound of her voice getting fainter, thankfully, as she moves further away.

"Whew!" Kenan breathes a sigh of relief. "Well, it was fun finding the true meaning of Christmas, but now it's time to talk about the New Year."

"The New Year," says Kel. "All right!" He removes his red Santa cap and replaces it with a festive party hat. He hands Kenan a noisemaker, as confetti begins pouring down on them from nowhere. "Whee!" shouts Kel. "Happy New Year! Come on, Kenan! Blow your noisemaker."

"Kel, wait a minute, man—"

"Blow your noisemaker, Kenan! It's New Year's!"

Grudgingly, Kenan gives a little blow on his noisemaker. Kel then reaches behind the curtain for a bottle of orange soda and two fancy tulip glasses. He pops open the orange soda bottle and pours a glass for Kenan and one for himself.

"Time to party!" shouts Kel.

"Hold on a minute, Kel. New Year's means more

than just celebrating and making noise. It's about change."

"Change?" says Kel, reaching into his pocket and pulling out some coins. "Let's see . . . I got two nickels and four pennies."

"Not that kind of change, *anteater*," says Kenan. "I'm talking about changing things in your life, and starting anew. You know. Makin' New Year's resolutions."

" 'New Year's resolutions'?" asks Kel. "Come on, Kenan. You know I'm not good with my hands that way. What are they made out of, anyway?"

Kenan explains to Kel that a New Year's resolution is not something you make with your hands, but with your *mind*. "It's something you just decide you're going to do from now on, or *not do any more*," says Kenan.

"Like what?" asks Kel, taking a huge swig of orange soda.

Kenan's eyes fixate on Kel's orange soda bottle. "Like bad habits," said Kenan.

"Bad habits?" says Kel. "Do I have any bad habits?"

"Well, yeah," says Kenan. "We all have bad habits. Like for instance, I sometimes fall asleep in front of my Aunt Louise."

"Oh, I get it," says Kel. "And I pick my head."

"Yeah, see, now *that's* a nasty habit," replies Kenan. "And I spend too much time at the zoo. That's kind of a bad habit."

"Yeah," agrees Kel, "and I run long distances with my eyes closed."

"That's a dangerous habit," remarks Kenan, still trying to lure Kel toward recognizing one particular bad habit.

"Well, it doesn't matter," Kel decides. "Every new year is always the same. I still got all my old bad habits, and the only thing that ever changes is, each year I get a few new ones."

"Well," says Kenan, "I think this New Year is going to be a little different."

"Whaddaya mean, Kenan?"

Kenan starts to walk away. "I don't know. I just think this New Year, we're gonna get rid of your worst bad habit of all." Kenan leaves the stage, leaving Kel standing there, dumbfounded with the turkeys again, who are now gobbling wildly over the coming of the new year.

"What are you talking about Kenan?" Kel shouts after him, clutching his bottle of orange soda. "How is this year going to be different? Kenan? Which one of my bad habits are we gonna get rid of? Kenan? Kenan!" Kel turns toward the empty seats once again. "Aw, here goes the New Year!" He throws his hands down in frustration and runs to catch up with Kenan.

"WHO LOVES ORANGE SODA?"

It was the first week of the New Year, and Kenan paced back and forth in the examining room while Kel was off getting X rays. Kenan was a good best friend. He was worried about Kel, who had hurt his ribs badly the night before. Evidently, while Kel had been bowling, he'd forgotten to let go of the ball. *It could happen to anybody,* thought Kenan. *On second thought, no, it couldn't.* The nurse walked in, carrying Kel's chart.

"Nurse! Miss Nurse?" asked Kenan. "How's Kel? Is he okay? Where is he?"

"The doctor is just finishing up Kel's X rays," replied the nurse. "He'll be right in."

Kenan looked around the examining room. It was a typical examining room. There was a skeleton in the corner, cabinets full of medical supplies, a counter with a sink, and a soft-covered examination table. Kenan picked up one of the doctor's instruments from a tray and tried to pluck one of his nose hairs. "Oww!" he shouted. He then picked up the reflex hammer, sat down on the examination table, and proceeded to test his own reflexes by hitting himself in the knee. Nothing happened. He tried again. Still, there was no reaction. He tried again and again and again. Nothing. Finally, he tried hitting a different part of his knee. It worked. His leg kicked up suddenly, and he knocked down the entire instrument tray. The metal tray and instruments made a huge crash as they hit the hard floor. Kenan sprung up from the table and quickly picked up the mess. It was then that Kel, his plaid button-down shirt open, revealing his heavily taped ribs, returned to the examining room with the nurse.

"Hey, Kel! So, what's wrong with your ribs?" Kenan asked.

"They're broken," replied Kel sadly.

"Broken ribs?" Kenan winced.

"I doubt your ribs are *broken*," said the nurse. "They're probably just bruised."

"Bruised?" Kenan seemed almost disappointed. "Aw, Kel man, you scared me for nothing!" Kenan, not thinking, casually whacked Kel in the ribs, causing him to scream and double over in pain. "Oops. Sorry."

The nurse instructed Kel to sit up on the examining table, and told him the doctor would be with him shortly. "Oh," she said, handing him a little plastic cup, "and you're going to need to fill this cup."

Kenan knew what that meant. Kel, obviously, did not.

"All right," said Kel. As the nurse walked out, he pulled a bottle of orange soda out of his pocket, opened it, and, humming happily, he filled the cup. He loved orange soda. It was his single favorite liquid on earth, and he always had a bottle with him. He sighed with pleasure after his first sip.

"Uh, Kel . . . ," said Kenan. "I don't think she meant to fill the cup up with *orange soda.*"

Dr. Goyter was a friendly-looking man. He looked very helpful and intelligent in his white lab coat and thin, wire-framed glasses. He came in the examining room, holding Kel's X rays, and introduced himself to Kenan. "Are you having a happy new year?" asked the doctor.

"Oh, yeah," said Kenan. "So far, it's been pretty good. How about yourself?"

"Oh, it's been a fine new year," said Dr. Goyter. "I'm making a lot of money, and I think I just bought a boat. It's a nice boat with—"

"What about my ribs?" Kel interrupted.

"Oh yeah," said Kenan. "So, how is he, Doc?"

"Well, let's have a look at Kel's X ray," said Dr. Goyter. He then hung up the X ray against the light box, displaying Kel's ribs. Strangely enough, according to the X ray, Kel's insides were a very bright *orange.* "Good grief! Look at that!" exclaimed Dr. Goyter.

"Oh, I knew it! My ribs are broken!" whined Kel.

"No, no . . . ," reassured the doctor. "Your ribs are just bruised, but . . ."

"But what?" asked Kenan, concerned about his confused friend.

"But Kel's insides . . . ," continued Dr. Goyter, ". . . appear to be . . . bright orange."

Kel looked sheepishly at his bottle of orange soda. Kenan explained to Dr. Goyter how much Kel loved orange soda.

"Is that true?" asked the doctor.

"Mmmmm-hmmmm," replied Kel, going into his routine. "I do I do I do I do-ooh!"

"But . . . ," began Doctor Goyter, "to turn your insides orange, you'd have to drink four or five gallons every day."

"Yeah, doc," said Kel. "So, what's your point?"

"Doc? Is Kel going to be okay?" asked Kenan.

"Oh, of course," replied Dr. Goyter, still flustered. "I'll just need to check a few things." The doctor called out toward the door. "Nurse! I'll need to take some blood!"

"Blood? *Noooooo!*" screamed Kel. Kenan held Kel's hand as the nurse walked back in with a huge hypodermic needle. Both Kenan and Kel took one look at it and fainted dead away.

"Well, that should make it easy," said Dr. Goyter, and he bent over Kel with the needle and proceeded to do his job.

A few minutes later, Kel was sitting back up on the examining table. Kenan gave him a pat on the back as the doctor took a good look at the contents of the syringe.

They were bright orange.

"What is it, doc?" asked Kenan.

"Well, it appears his blood is made up largely of . . . orange soda," said Dr. Goyter in a rather puzzled tone.

"What does that mean?" asked Kel.

Dr. Goyter put the syringe down on the counter and walked over to Kel. "Kel, I'm not quite sure," began the doctor, "but my professional opinion is that you're drinking a little too much orange soda. You need to quit."

"But what would I drink?" asked Kel.

The doctor suggested water. Kel cringed. Kenan just shook his head.

"Look, Kel, this is a perfect time to give up orange soda," said Dr. Goyter. "It's the new year. You can make it your number one New Year's resolution."

" 'New Year's resolution'?" repeated Kel.

"Yes," said the doctor. "You simply promise yourself that this year, you will not drink any more orange soda. Go ahead, Kel. Say it: 'This year, I, Kel Mitchell, will quit drinking orange soda, starting right this minute.' "

"Oh," said Kel, annoyed. "So you think just because you're a doctor and we both have the same name, you can make me quit drinking orange soda? I don't think so."

Kenan and Dr. Goyter rolled their eyes in frustration.

Kel's ribs were hurting, so Kenan helped him into Rigby's Grocery Store and helped him lie down on the counter on his back.

"You need anything?" asked Kenan.

"Well, maybe just a little . . ."

Kenan knew what Kel was going to say, and he went to the drink section to get a bottle of orange soda. Meanwhile, Chris Potter, carrying a huge box of Lulu's Mango Jelly in front of his face, staggered in from the back room.

"Kenan!" Chris shouted. "Help me with this box! It's heavy and I can't see!" He had to set it down quickly. Unable to see Kel lying on the counter, Chris slammed the box right down on Kel's bruised ribs.

"Yaaaaghhhh!" screamed Kel, jumping up off the counter. Kel's scream scared Chris so much that Chris screamed too.

"Aw, look!" complained Chris. "You 'be-broke' my mango jelly jars!"

"Don't yell at him!" said Kenan, rushing to his friend's aid. "His ribs are all 'be-bruised'!" Kenan handed Kel his bottle of orange soda, then he told Chris all about the visit to the doctor's office. "You should've seen his X rays. His insides are bright orange."

"They weren't *that* orange," argued Kel.

"Aww, man!" replied Kenan. "Your insides are more orange than a Nickelodeon logo."

"So?" said Kel.

"*So,* maybe you should quit drinking orange soda," suggested Chris, as he took the orange soda bottle from Kel and went into the back room.

"Maybe I will!" shouted Kel defiantly.

"Ha!" said Kenan.

"What do you mean by 'ha'?" asked Kel.

"I mean, you couldn't make that New Year's resolution if your life depended on it," said Kenan as he took off his black leather jacket and put on his blue Rigby's apron.

"I can quit drinking orange soda any time I want," declared Kel.

Kenan didn't think so. "Kel, you couldn't go one day without drinking orange soda, let alone a whole lifetime."

"I could go for a whole *week* without drinking orange soda!" claimed Kel.

"False!" shouted Kenan. It sounded like he didn't think Kel could do it.

"You wanna bet?" Kel challenged.

"You got a bet!" said Kenan. "The bet is . . . you have to go an entire week without taking one sip of orange soda. If you lose, then . . ." He hesitated, thinking hard.

"Then what?" asked Kel.

Kenan knew he was going to win, so he had to think of something especially humiliating for Kel to do. "Then you gotta stand on this counter, in the middle of the daytime, singing the national anthem, wearing nothing but a lady's nightgown." *There!* thought Kenan. *That oughtta do it.*

"Okay, okay," agreed Kel. "But if I win, then *you* have to do it!"

"You're on!" said Kenan, and they shook hands.

Kenan then reached down under the counter and pulled out two bottles of orange soda. "Let's drink to it," he said.

"Let's drink to it," agreed Kel.

Kenan took a sip, and Kel was just about to drink when he realized what he was doing and stopped himself.

"Awwww!" moaned Kel.

"Mmmmm!" taunted Kenan, with a satisfied smile. "That's goooood orange soda."

Kel wanted that orange soda so bad he could taste it. Instead, he just stood there and glared at Kenan.

When Kel sat down to dinner at the Rockmores' kitchen table, the first thing Sheryl offered him was some orange soda.

"Oh, that's okay," said Kel. "No orange soda for me."

Roger and Kyra gasped. Sheryl was so stunned that she dropped a tray of silverware.

"No orange soda?" asked Roger.

"I'll go call nine-one-one!" said Kyra, leaping from her seat and heading for the phone.

Kenan told Kyra to put the phone down and reassured his family that everything was all right.

"Yeah. We made a bet," said Kel. "I bet Kenan I could go a whole week without drinking orange soda."

There was a moment of shocked silence, then the Rockmores burst out laughing.

"Hey, come on!" shouted Kel. "I can do it!"

"Oh no you can't," teased Sheryl. Poor Kel. Even Kenan's sweet mother was in on the fun at his expense.

Roger then reached into the fridge and brought out a huge bottle of orange soda. He smiled at Kel, opened the top, and guzzled it down. "Kel!" sang Roger in a strange voice. "Woo-hoo! Look at me! I'm a man drinking orange soda! Mmmmmmmmmm-mmmmm, that's goooood!"

Kel's mouth was watering. Why were they all doing this to him? At least Kyra remained true to him. She kept it no secret that she always loved Kel, and she wasn't going to abandon him now. "Now, you all stop being mean to Kel!" she ordered.

"Yes," added Sheryl. "It's not nice to tease Kel by drinking orange soda in front of him."

"Thanks, Mrs. Rockmore," said Kel. He was relieved. Finally there was some compassion in the room from an adult.

Kenan, however, wasn't through teasing his friend. After all, he had a bet to win. He walked over, took the orange soda bottle from his dad, and headed for the sink. "Yeah. In fact, just so Kel won't be tempted, why don't we . . ." To Kel's horror, Kenan began pouring the entire bottle of orange soda down the drain. ". . . pour this whole bottle of sweet, bubbly orangey goodness right down the drain."

Kel screamed from the pain of watching his beloved orange soda go to waste.

"Bye-bye, orange soda!" said Kenan.

Kel pointed his spoon at Kenan. "You're a sick, sick young man."

"Yeah," said Kenan. "And I'm gonna win the bet, too."

It was not a fun dinner at the Rockmores' for Kel, and it just kept getting worse. Kenan and his dad leaned across the table and began chanting *"Kel's gonna loo-oose! Kel's gonna loo-oose!"* over and over again. He couldn't take it anymore, and he finally got up from the table and went into the living room.

Sometimes, even the best of friends can get on each other's nerves, and this was definitely the case with Kel. He wished he had never made that bet with Kenan, as he paced back and forth across the Rockmores' living room floor.

Kenan, on the other hand, wanted to win that bet more than anything. And he knew how to do it, too. He followed Kel in the living room with a bottle of orange soda and spoke to him very gently. "Kel, don't be upset, buddy. Come on now. Why don't you just take a little sip of orange soda and get it over with?"

Kenan then handed Kel the bottle. Kel stared at it for what seemed like an eternity.

"No!" said Kel finally, and he took the full bottle of orange heaven and tossed it across the Rockmore living room as hard as he could. Well, it was about that precise moment that Roger decided to come out into the living room to see what was going on. It was a bad decision for Roger. For the third time in this book, Roger was nailed in the head—this time, by a flying orange soda bottle.

Roger dropped to the floor like a rock. Kel raced for the door, but Kenan stopped him.

"You're gonna stay right here where I can keep my eye on you," said Kenan. It made sense. How else would Kenan know whether or not Kel was sneaking himself some orange soda?

"What?" said Kel. "You don't trust me?"

Kenan thought for a moment. "Let me see . . . uhh . . . *nope!*" Kel was insulted. Kenan told him he could sleep in his room.

"Okay," said Kel. "I'll stay right here, so you can watch me *not* drink orange soda."

They taunted each other about who was going to be singing songs while wearing a lady's nighty, then went upstairs to bed.

Kel was in his pajamas, tucking himself into his sleeping bag, next to Kenan's bed, when Kenan walked in with a bottle of orange soda. He set it down on the floor, next to Kel.

"Just in case you get thirsty during the middle of the night, you can have some of this," laughed Kenan.

"Yeah, laugh it up," said Kel. Kenan left the room for a moment, and Kel sat up and stared at his friend turned bitter enemy—the bottle of orange soda. "Who loves orange soda?" Kel asked himself, mocking his own famous orange soda routine. "Kel doesn't love orange soda. Is it true? Mmmm-hmmm! I don't I don't I don't I doh-on't!" It sounded as if he was trying to convince himself. Then, Kel glared at the bottle and knocked it over with his foot. He got up, grabbed it, and started shaking it angrily. "Stupid orange soda. Who do you think you are? Acting all orange and carbonated! I hate you! Why don't you just get out of here!" Then Kel did something he never ever thought he would do to orange soda. He tossed it on the floor. All the shaking had built up the pressure in the bottle, and the soda began to fizz. Kel froze with sorrow as he looked at his once beloved orange soda, lying there on the floor, leaking. Suddenly, he realized what he had done, and raced over to the bottle. He plugged up the leak with his hand. He hugged it and kissed it as if it was his baby son. "I didn't mean it!" cried Kel. "I've always loved you! Oh, sweet, sweet orange soda!" He cradled the bottle of orange soda in his arms, wrapped it gently in his blanket, climbed into his sleeping bag, and cuddled with it until he fell asleep.

That night was not an easy one for Kel. He tossed and turned, and mumbled to himself in his sleep. He was having a bizarre dream. He was dreaming he was wealthy, and he owned a big Jacuzzi filled with orange soda. Roger Rockmore was his butler, dressed in an orange tuxedo.

"Mister Kel? Your orange Jacuzzi is ready," said Roger.

"Thank you, Rockmore," said Kel in a wealthy, dignified voice. Roger then helped Kel off with his orange robe, and Kel, in his orange bathing suit, climbed in the frothing orange soda Jacuzzi, an orange soda waterfall pouring into it.

"How's the orange soda, sir?" asked Roger the butler.

"Wonderful," said Kel.

"Are you thirsty, sir?" asked Roger.

"Why, yes, I am." Kel clapped his hands twice. "Oh, beverage boy!" In one second, Kenan the beverage boy arrived on the scene wearing an orange busboy's outfit, carrying a tray holding one tall glass of orange soda.

"I would like some orange soda," said Kel.

"Very good, Mister Kel," Kenan replied. He handed Kel the glass of orange soda, the straw sticking straight up. Kel tried to take a sip, but much to his disappointment, no orange soda would come out. Kel became hysterical. He tried frantically shaking the glass, turning it upside down and all around, but the orange soda simply stayed in the glass.

"What? . . . What's going on? My orange soda! It won't come out!"

Kenan and Roger began laughing maniacally.

"Stop laughing! There's nothing funny about this! Help me!" screamed Kel. "Heeeelllllp!"

"Sure, we'll get you some help," said Kenan, in a sinister tone.

"Orange Monster!" called Roger.

Before Kel knew it, a strange-looking orange monster raced onto the scene, jumped into the Jacuzzi, and began wrestling him. He had an orange face, floppy, stringy orange hair, orange arms and legs, and orange tentacles coming out all over.

"Yaaaaahhhhhh!" screamed Kel, absolutely terrified. Kenan and Roger simply continued to laugh as the orange monster pummeled Kel.

Everyone knows the best part about a bad dream is waking up from it. So, one could imagine how fortunate Kel felt when he woke up the next morning and realized he was *not,* in fact, being attacked by the orange monster. "Whew! What a relief!" He glanced around and recognized that he was in Kenan's room, and that Kenan wasn't an evil beverage boy, and that Roger wasn't his wicked butler. But when he felt his pajamas to make sure he hadn't been in a Jacuzzi filled with orange soda, he got quite a scare. He was soaked! There was orange soda all over him. He jumped up and found the bottle of orange soda he'd fallen asleep with. It was empty. It had leaked all over him during the night. Kel screamed long and loud.

Immediately, Kenan jumped out of bed and turned on the lights. "Wh—— what happened?" he asked, his eyes adjusting to the light. Then Kenan saw the empty orange soda bottle. He looked at the white T-shirt Kel wore under his pajamas. It had a giant orange soda stain. "A-ha!" Kenan shouted. "You *did* drink the orange soda!"

"No, no, no I didn't! It just spilled!" explained Kel.

"Ha!" scoffed Kenan, straightening in his black-and-white checkered pajamas.

"I swear!" Kel swore.

"Then let me see your tongue," demanded Kenan. With that, Kenan picked up a flashlight, shined it in Kel's mouth, and saw that his tongue wasn't orange. "Well, your tongue isn't orange . . . yet," said Kenan in an ominous tone.

Kel was vindicated. "See? I told you I could go a whole day without drinking orange soda."

Kenan reminded Kel that it was just one day, and that there were six more to go.

"You're gonna lose," teased Kel.

"I think not," replied Kenan, laughing confidently.

It had been three whole days, and Kel had not taken one sip of orange soda. He had never gone that long without orange soda, and he was beginning to lose his mind. He just stood there in the corner of Rigby's Grocery Store, shivering and twitching.

"Kenan," said Chris, as he was wheeling in boxes of orange soda, "Why don't you call off the bet? Look at him!" Chris pointed to the feeble Kel, who was still shaking and quivering near the produce section.

"This is good for him," Kenan replied, as he stacked bottles of orange soda for a display that read SPECIAL ORANGE SODA: 2 FOR 1.

" 'Good'?" Chris couldn't believe how mean Kenan was being. "Give him an orange soda, already! He's suffering over there."

Kenan told Chris that Kel could certainly have an orange soda. That is, if he wanted to break his New

Year's resolution, and more importantly, lose the bet and sing the national anthem in a lady's nightie.

Meanwhile, Kel took an orange and stuck the whole thing in his mouth, peel and all.

"Kel! What are you doing?" yelled Kenan.

Kel removed the orange from his mouth. "Sucking on an orange," he explained, grimacing with frustration. He was looking tired and unkempt. His backward baseball cap was tilted to one side, and his brown jacket was falling off one shoulder. "Aw, it's not working!" he shouted, and he angrily threw the orange into the dairy section, knocking over a bunch of milk cartons.

Chris wasn't angry with him, though. He felt bad for Kel. "Kel, listen, if you want to get over your orange soda habit, I know how you can do it," offered Chris.

"How?" asked the desperate Kel.

"Go see a hypnotist," Chris suggested.

"A hyp-no-tist?" Kel had never heard the word before.

Chris swore by hypnotists. He told Kel that if it wasn't for his hypnotist, he would never have gotten over his fear of sandwiches.

"You're afraid of sandwiches?" Kenan laughed.

"Not anymore," said Chris. "Thanks to Doctor Vermin." Chris went into his wallet and gave Kel Dr. Vermin's business card. "You should go see him."

"I will!" shouted Kel. Suddenly infused with a glimmer of hope, he started for the door.

"Then I'm going with you," announced Kenan.

"But, Kenan, you have work to do here," said Chris.

"No thank you," replied Kenan, and he followed Kel out the door.

Chris just stood there in his gray Rigby's manager's apron, shook his head, and mumbled bad stuff about Kenan.

The receptionist at Dr. Vermin's office gave Kel a form to fill out, and told him to write down the reason he'd come to see the hypnotist. Kenan and Kel sat down on a couch in the waiting room next to a peculiar woman in an odd-looking hat. She sat there with her little white Pekinese.

Kel busily filled out his form while Kenan admired the dog. "Wow, cute dog," said Kenan.

"Oh, thank you," replied the woman. "I'm Mrs. Felsenthal and his name is Dustin. He's here to see the hypnotist."

Kel looked up from his paperwork. "Wait a minute. Doctor Vermin hypnotizes pets, too?"

"Oh, yes. Doctor Vermin hypnotizes people, cats, dogs, lizards, salmon, you name it," said Mrs. Felsenthal.

"Well, what's wrong with your dog?" asked Kenan.

Mrs. Felsenthal explained that Dustin was supposed to be an attack dog, but all he did was lie there. In fact, that's exactly what Dustin was doing right now on the couch. "I'm hoping Doctor Vermin can hypnotize him into being more aggressive and ferocious," she said.

The receptionist came out into the waiting room and took both Kel's and Mrs. Felsenthal's forms. "Kel, you're going to be in Room A. Mrs. Felsenthal, you can take Dustin into Room B. The hypnotist will see you shortly."

"Good luck, Kel and Dustin," said Kenan, as he waved to his friend and the lethargic dog.

Kenan cared about Kel. There was no doubt about it. They were best friends, and he would never want to cause him any real harm. But when two teenage boys make a bet, no matter how close they are, winning that bet becomes all that matters. So, Kenan sneaked around the corner of the hallway in Dr. Vermin's clinic. He glanced around to make sure no one was there. Sitting in plastic holders on the outside of the doors to Rooms A and B were the forms that Kel and Mrs. Felsenthal had filled out. Quickly, Kenan switched the forms. He laughed a nasty, mischievous laugh, and snuck quietly back into the waiting room.

Kel was waiting at Dr. Vermin's desk when the doctor finally walked in.

"Well, hello there, Dustin," greeted Dr. Vermin as he glanced at the form in his hand.

"Dustin?" said Kel. "My name is—"

But Dr. Vermin was in a hurry. He was a dignified, intelligent-looking man with glasses, a beard, and mustache. He wore a mysterious-looking black suit over a black shirt. He walked over to his desk and sat opposite Kel. "Now, now, Dustin. I realize you may feel a bit uneasy seeing a hypnotist for the first time . . ."

"Yeah, I'm a little nervous," replied Kel, "but my name isn't—"

Dr. Vermin interrupted again as he studied the form more carefully. "Well, I see you have an interesting problem, Dustin."

"I sure do," replied Kel, "but my na——"

"Well, not to worry," interrupted Dr. Vermin a third time. "We'll have you acting more ferocious in no time."

"Ferocious? But my problem is that I love orange—"

"Just sit back, Dustin, and watch my whirling thing," instructed Dr. Vermin. He then placed a large, strange-looking disk on his desk. It was white with thick lines spiraling around it, kind of like a giant peppermint, except the lines were black. He pointed his whirling thing at Kel and turned it on. It spun around rapidly, and the lines became bigger, then smaller, then bigger again.

Kel looked right at it, quickly becoming mesmerized.

"Now, when I count to three, you will go into a trance," said Dr. Vermin. "One . . . two . . ."

"Boy, you're crazy," laughed Kel. "You can never get me to—"

". . . three," continued Dr. Vermin.

Kel instantly went into a trance. He looked at the spiral, his mouth contorted to one side, his eyes wide open.

"Now, Dustin," began Dr. Vermin calmly, "you will no longer be afraid to be aggressive and vicious. In fact, whenever you hear a bell, you will become a fearless, ferocious beast!"

"Fearless, ferocious . . . beastus . . . ," repeated Kel, in a trance.

"Yes, that's right, Dustin . . . excellent . . . whenever you hear a bell . . . ferocious . . . ," said Dr. Vermin.

Kel muttered Dr. Vermin's words to himself as he continued to helplessly watch the whirling disk.

"How'd it go?" asked Chris, from behind the counter at Rigby's. Kenan and Kel had just walked in. "Did it work?"

"I don't know," replied Kel.

It was then that old Mrs. Quagmeyer entered the store. "Excuse me?"

"Yes, Mrs. Quagmeyer?" said Kenan as he put his blue Rigby's apron back on.

Mrs. Quagmeyer had come in for nine jars of extra chunky mayonnaise. It was a lot of jars, so Chris and Kenan had to go get them from the back room. That left Kel alone in the store with Mrs. Quagmeyer.

"Hey, what's shaking, Quagmeyer?" asked Kel.

"I need change for a dollar," said Mrs. Quagmeyer. "Will you get it for me, please?" Mrs. Quagmeyer went into her purse and handed Kel a dollar bill.

"All right," said Kel, taking the dollar. "I'll just get it out of the cash register." Even though Kel didn't work at Rigby's, he was there all the time, and he felt it was perfectly okay for him to make change for Mrs. Quagmeyer. He reached over the counter to the cash register, and hit a button to open it. *Ding!* It was the little bell that goes off whenever cash registers are opened.

Suddenly, Kel looked as if he had become possessed. It was the same look he had had when he was in the hypnotist's office in a trance. He immediately began to snarl and growl.

"Is something wrong?" asked Mrs. Quagmeyer.

Something must have been very wrong, because Kel was barking like a vicious dog. He stood in front of Mrs. Quagmeyer, growling and showing his teeth. Then, he got on all fours, and began chasing her around the store.

"Holy shivers!" shouted Mrs. Quagmeyer, as Kel chased her past the orange soda display, around the potato chips, and back to the front counter. "Help! Help! Down, boy!" she screamed, when, suddenly, the phone rang. Another bell, of sorts, and just as soon as Kel's ferocious, canine behavior started, it abruptly ended. Kenan came out from the back and answered the phone, while Chris carefully set the nine jars of mayonnaise on the counter for Mrs. Quagmeyer.

"Keep your stinking mayonnaise!" screamed Mrs. Quagmeyer. "Weirdos!" She carefully sidestepped Kel, then left in a huff.

"Come on, Kenan. Let's go put these jars of mayonnaise back," said Chris, shaking his head, puzzled at her abrupt departure. Once again, they left Kel alone at the front of the store.

A lady walked in with six nine-year-old kids, wearing red and blue band costumes, and holding various musical instruments.

"Hello," she said to Kel, since he was the only one there. "I'm the band instructor at Brimfield Elementary School. Our bus broke down, and I was wondering if I could use the phone."

Kel didn't see why not, and he directed her to the phone. He looked at one of the kids—a boy holding a trumpet. "So," said Kel, trying to be friendly to the young man, "you in a band?"

"No, I just use this to make toast," said the sarcastic little boy, pointing to his trumpet.

Kel was offended. "Well! I never!"

"I play the triangle," volunteered a cute little girl.

"Oh yeah?" asked Kel.

"Yeah, watch!" she said, and she banged once on her metal triangle, making a loud dinging sound. Another bell. Kel instantly went back into his hypnotic trance and turned into a mean, aggressive dog again. While their instructor finished up her phone call, Kel snarled and growled at the kids.

"What's with this guy?" asked a boy.

"Okay, kids," said the band instructor, returning from making her call, "a taxi is coming to pick us all up in just a few—"

Kel turned around and pounced on her before she could finish her sentence. She screamed and ran away. Kel, thinking he was a wild dog, got back on all fours and chased her around the store, knocking everything

105

down in his path. The kids scrambled to get out of his way. Kenan and Chris ran out from the back room and witnessed the incident.

"Kel!" screamed Chris. "What are you doing?" He ran out to try to stop him.

"Wow!" said Kenan with an ear-to-ear smile. "That hypnotism stuff really works! I could be sure of one thing: if Dustin liked orange soda before, I'll bet he hates it now!"

Kel continued barking and growling as he tried to bite the instructor's skirt.

"Get him off me!" she screamed.

"Kel! Down! Down, boy!" yelled Chris.

Kel lunged at Chris, as the band instructor and the kids escaped unharmed. Kel then jumped on Chris's back and tried to wrestle him to the ground.

"Kenan, help! He's gone insane!"

Kenan had an idea. He went to get a dog dish from the shelf and grabbed a bottle of orange soda. He quickly poured the orange soda in the dish, set it on the counter, and whistled for Kel to come and get it. "Here ya go, boy!" called Kenan.

"Woof!" said Kel, and he got off of Chris, jumped on top of the counter on all fours, and began lapping up the orange soda like a thirsty dog drinks water. It took some doing, but Kenan had done it. He'd gotten Kel to drink orange soda before the week was over. Kenan had won the bet. Or had he? The phone rang again, and Kel came right out of his trance, snapping back to human form.

"Hey, guys," said Kel, having no idea what had just happened.

Chris picked the phone up, told whoever it was to call back later, and hung up. "Kel, what's the matter with you?" he demanded.

Kel didn't know what Chris was talking about. He'd been in a trance, and didn't remember a thing about being a dog. He put his hand to his face and felt it was wet with orange soda. "Why is there orange soda on my face?" he asked.

Kenan celebrated. "Ha! Because you drunk it! Out of a dog dish! And that means you lose the bet! Now, put on a lady's nightie, get on that counter, and start singing!"

Kel, of course, had no recollection of drinking anything out of a dog dish, and he denied it.

"Yes, you did," said Chris. "Right out of that dish. You were acting like a becrazed dog!"

Kel was more confused than ever. "Why would I act like a 'becrazed' dog?"

" 'Cuz I switched the forms at the hypnotist's office," laughed Kenan. "You lose the bet!"

"No!" Kel protested. "You cheated!"

"So?" said Kenan. "You still drank the soda. You lose."

" 'Fraid not!"

" 'Fraid so!"

The argument ensued. Who really won the bet? After all, Kel never *consciously* drank any orange soda, although he did actually drink orange soda. But, Kel argued, Kenan cheated him into doing it against his will.

"Why don't we let Chris decide who lost?" suggested Kenan.

It was fine with Kel. "Whatever Chris decides, goes!" said Kel, confident that Chris, being the fair man that he was, would surely see it his way.

Chris thought hard. It was not a job he wanted, but he had to make the decision that was the most fair to all parties concerned. Suddenly, a faint smile could be seen on Chris's face.

There were so many customers at Rigby's that one might think they were having a huge sale. Strangely, though, they were all gathered in front of the counter. Chris stood in front of the small crowd.

"Ladies and gentlemen . . . ," said Chris, ". . . Kenan and Kel!"

Chris pointed to the top of the counter, where both Kenan *and* Kel were standing in their bathrobes. They removed their robes to reveal cute, frilly lady's night-gowns underneath. The crowd pointed and laughed. The boys then began to sing:

"Oh say can you see, by the dawn's early light, What so proudly we hailed . . ."

Chris happily acted as conductor, as Kenan and Kel, looking miserable but pretty in their nighties, sang loudly and clearly to their adoring fans.

A BRAND NEW HOLIDAY?

Kenan and Kel emerge once again through the red curtain, still wearing their nighties. Kel carries a large cage for his turkeys.

"I'm taking my turkeys home!" sings Kel.

"You're a lucky guy," says Kenan.

"Well," says Kel, "I didn't keep my New Year's resolotion."

"Resolution," corrects Kenan.

"Yeah, I didn't keep that, either. I started drinking orange soda the minute we finished our song."

"Well, *water beetle,* I think we still got ourselves a pretty good New Year's resolution," says Kenan.

"What's that?" asks Kel, as he gathers up his turkeys and leads them into their new cage by scattering bread crumbs and sunflower seeds.

"My new New Year's resolution is to never make a bet with you again. How about you, Kel?"

"Okay," says Kel. "I'll make a New Year's resolution

109

every year. My new New Year's resolution is to only pick my head on Wednesdays and Fridays. Next year, it'll be to stop going to school so much. The year after that, it'll be to chew more gum. The year after that . . ."

Kenan gives Kel a long peculiar stare. "Hellooooo?" calls Kenan, knocking his fist on the side of Kel's head. "Anybody home?"

"Are you trying to tell me my head is shaped like a house?" asks Kel, somewhat insulted, but not for the reason he *should* be insulted.

Kenan shakes his head and puts his arm around his confused best friend. "Well, Kel, we made it through another holiday season."

"Yeah, and so did my turkeys," says Kel with pride.

"Ya know, *butter bean,* the holidays are sometimes a pain in the behind, but they're pretty darn special."

"I'm gonna miss them, Kenan! Now we have no really big holididdie-ays to look forward to for a long time. We should have one more big one right in the middle of the year, like somewhere around June thirty-third."

"Kel, there is no June thirty-third."

"Oh yeah," remembers Kel. "June is one of those months with only thirty-two days."

Kenan rolls his eyes and mumbles to himself. *Kel doesn't know how many days are in a month,* Kenan thinks, *but he does make a good point. There* should *be a new holiday to look forward to. Why wait all the way to the end of November?* "You're right, Kel," says Kenan, finally.

"I am?" asks Kel, somewhat shocked. "I've never actually been right before. Hey! It feels all tingly."

"Yeah, well, enjoy it while you can, because it's not going to happen too often," cautions Kenan. "Now, think hard. What could be a new big holiday we could have to look forward to?"

Kenan and Kel think hard.

"How about Christmas?" asks Kel.

"We just had that one, *sucker fish!* Now keep thinking!"

Kenan and Kel pace back and forth on the stage. Suddenly, Kenan stops in his tracks and raises his index finger in the air. "I got it!" he announces victoriously.

"Don't worry, Kenan. I'll take you to the doctor," assures Kel.

"Noooo, Kel. I don't have a disease. I got an idea for a new holiday."

"What is it?" asks Kel, excited.

"It's called . . . 'KelKenan's Day,'" replies Kenan, smiling.

"'KelKenan's Day,'" repeats Kel. "I like it. What's it for?"

Kenan hadn't really thought that far ahead. He struggles for a response. "It's to celebrate the first time my daddy threw you out of our house, and I talked him into letting you stay."

"Cool! When is KelKenan's Day?"

"Tomorrow!" decides Kenan.

"Then, I guess that makes today KelKenan's Eve!" Kel realizes.

"You're right!" exclaims Kenan. "We gotta get ready, *possum pouch!*"

"Yeah!" Kel starts to move quickly in either direction, then realizes he has no idea what to do. "How do we get ready?"

"Well," says Kenan, "there's the twenty-three-foot pizza to prepare . . ."

"There's the dirt to throw over the furniture . . . ," adds Kel.

"Yep," agrees Kenan. "And then we gotta hang pictures of people wearing light blue."

"Uh-huh," says Kel. "And don't forget to throw pineapple slices at your daddy's head."

"Wasn't gonna," replies Kenan. "And then, we have to get the money shrub and decorate it with breakfast cereals. Oh yeah, and I almost forgot. We have to get the 'you-know-what.'"

"The 'you-know-what'?"

"Yeah. I'd better go change out of my nightie and pick that up right now. But first, I'm going to say good-bye to the people." Kenan turns and faces the empty chairs in front of the stage. "Bye everyone! Happy holidays. And, especially, Happy KelKenan's Day."

"Yeah," adds Kel. "And we hope your holidays will always be full of good food, fun, family and fffff . . ." Kel turns to Kenan. "What's another good word that starts with f, Kenan?"

"Fragilations," offers Kenan, rolling his eyes.

"Yeah!" shouts Kel. "Fragilations! May all your

holidays be full of good food, fun, family and fragilations!"

"Okay, Kel, now I gotta go to get the you-know-what, or KelKenan's Day is going to be ruined. See ya later." And with that, Kenan walks away, leaving Kel standing there in his nightie, holding his cage full of turkeys, dumbfounded and confused.

"But, Kenan! What's the you-know-what? And why is KelKenan's Day gonna be ruined if we don't get a you-know-what? Kenan! Kenan? Keeeeeenan!" Kel turns and faces the empty seats, and throws up his hands in frustration. "Aw, here it goes!" Kel takes his turkeys and runs off after Kenan.

ABOUT THE AUTHOR

STEVE FREEMAN has written for several Nickelode-on shows including *All That* and *Kenan and Kel*. He has no idea how old he is, where he comes from, how he got there, or what he had for breakfast this morning.